CHEERLEADERS

#19

MAKING IT

SUSAN BLAKE

SCHOLASTIC INC.
New York Toronto London Auckland Sydney

ISBN 0-590-40189-0

12 11 10 9 8 7 6 5 4 3 2 1   7   6 7 8 9/8 0 1/9

Printed in the U.S.A.   01

CHEERLEADERS

MAKING IT

CHEERLEADERS

CHAPTER

Mary Ellen Kirkwood sat on the bed in the little bedroom she shared with her younger sister Gemma, and stared at the dozen or so glossy photographs laid out in front of her. It was getting late, and her economics textbook and her English homework — two short stories and some poems to be read — were stacked on the corner of the desk under the window. If she didn't get to it tonight, she might as well not go to class tomorrow. And if she didn't go to class, Ardith Engborg would call her into the office for another one of the little "talks" they seemed to be having more and more frequently. Mrs. Engborg would look stern and remind Mary Ellen how important it was for the captain of the Tarenton High Varsity Cheerleading Squad to set a good example with her schoolwork. And Mary Ellen would look

1

penitent and say that she was definitely going to do better from now on. She was going to *concentrate*.

The trouble was that there was just too much to think about these days. There was schoolwork and cheerleading and all the senior-year activities at Tarenton High. And of course there was Patrick Henley and. . . .

At the thought of Patrick Henley, Mary Ellen closed her eyes dizzily, remembering what had happened earlier that afternoon. She had been standing beside her locker after class when Patrick had come up behind her and put his powerful arms around her and pulled her close against him and. . . .

At the thought of Patrick's warm kiss on her neck, Mary Ellen shivered and opened her eyes wide again. Tonight she was *not* going to think about Patrick Henley. Tonight she was going to think about her portfolio. *That* was far more important than Patrick. After all, her portfolio was her ticket out of Tarenton, to a modeling career in the big, wide world out there. Her ticket to a future that was bright with sparkling lights and popping flashbulbs, and filled with the sound of appreciative applause. These days, Mary Ellen's present was filled with compelling thoughts about the future. The future, in fact, seemed to be all she had time to think about.

Her portfolio. Mary Ellen looked at the photographs scattered on the pink chenille spread. She sighed. Really, they were very nice photographs. Patrick had done the best he could — which was pretty good, actually, considering everything. Patrick was the official Tarenton High photographer, and his pictures of ball games and track meets and school events regularly appeared on the sports and society pages of the local newspaper, as well as in Tarenton High's school paper and yearbook. Everybody said that Patrick's pictures were as good as any of the other photos in the Tarenton newspaper. But that wasn't saying a whole lot, in Mary Ellen's personal opinion, since the Tarenton newspaper was about as rinky-dink as the town itself. Tarenton. The little town where nothing exciting *ever* happened.

Mary Ellen picked up one of the photographs and studied it with a resigned sigh. It showed a beautiful, bright-eyed, ponytailed cheerleader, bouncing high in the air, back perfectly arched, arms over her head and skirt flaring out gracefully around slim legs. Patrick's photograph — in fact, *all* of his photographs — looked like a poster for the All-American Girl contest. Miss High School Cheerleader, U.S.A. Nearly all the photographs in her portfolio were alike: more cheerleading shots, a few photos Patrick had taken at Marnie's boutique where she modeled on Saturdays, pictures of her out at the lake wearing a bathing suit, another photograph of her dressed in a formal for a school dance. They were all nice photographs, and up to a few weeks ago, she had been thrilled with them, but. . . .

But Mary Ellen's recent experiences with professional modeling — the horrible trip to the modeling agency in New York, and her brief and

3

unfortunate excursion to Chicago with Pres Tilford's friend Blake — had been rather sobering. In fact, remembering the way the woman in the New York modeling agency had looked at her, Mary Ellen could feel her face getting hot. She would never forget that look, the look that said, "We have a lot of your type." The point was all too clear. All-American girls from small towns, with small-town experience and that small-town look about them, were a dime a dozen.

And the Chicago experience had been equally awful. How in the world had she thought she knew how to read a modeling contract? Where had she gotten the idea that she could *manage* herself without an agent? But through all the awfulness, she had learned something very valuable. She had learned that if she was going to attract any serious attention in Chicago or New York, she was going to have to take charge of herself — or let somebody take charge for her.

Mary Ellen sighed. Yes, that's exactly what she needed. Somebody who could take charge for her. An agent, or a manager, or somebody like that. Somebody who could give her some suggestions, somebody who *knew* the modeling business. Of course, there was Mrs. Gunderson, her employer at Marnie's, who had been a model for years. Mrs. Gunderson had already been helpful. But her modeling experience was long past, and Mrs. Gunderson, nice as she was, was out of touch with what was going on in the big cities.

No, what she needed was someone up-to-date, someone who knew something about the business, someone who could help her make the very most of what she had. She had learned in New York and Chicago that looking sexy and beautiful all by itself — no matter how sexy and beautiful she looked — just wasn't going to cut it. Sure, it was okay when you were in high school to have that cheerleader image. In fact, it was more than okay — it was absolutely wonderful! Being captain of the Tarenton Varsity Cheerleading Squad was something she had dreamed of ever since kindergarten. But once she had graduated from Tarenton High and was out in the real world, Mary Ellen knew that she was going to have to *be* different: She was going to have to look different and act different. And she needed somebody to help her figure out how to get that way — in a hurry.

At that moment the phone rang. There was a brief scuffle of feet in the hallway, and after a minute Gemma stuck her head in the door. "Melon, it's Pres," she said. "He wants to talk to you." She looked at the mess of photos on her sister's bed. "Are you going to be at that all night?" she demanded. "We have a field trip tomorrow and I wanted to get to bed early."

Mary Ellen ignored her sister. She hated to be called Melon, even when Gemma did it. Taking her time, she carefully gathered up the scattered photographs and put them neatly into the big brown folder. In spite of the fact that Pres was one of her co-cheerleaders and they saw one another every day at school and at practice, he didn't call very often, and she didn't want him to think that she didn't have anything else to do but run to the phone to talk to him.

For a few minutes, while she was putting the photos away in the bottom drawer of her desk, Mary Ellen gave in to the interesting speculation that Pres might be going to ask her for a date. Once the two of them had had a brief and rather exciting romantic fling, but nothing permanent or very special had come of it. They'd just drifted along, feeling sort of warm and companionable toward each other, like two good friends.

Mary Ellen frowned thoughtfully. Maybe she should pay more attention to Pres, she reflected, as she went to the phone out in the hallway where it was shared by the whole Kirkwood family. Pres, with his family's business connections, could be very helpful to her. And anyway, Preston Tilford III was a great deal more suited to her tastes and ambitions than Patrick Henley. In fact, the difference between the two could be summed up very simply: It was the difference between a Porsche and a garbage truck. Mary Ellen picked up the phone with a thoughtful look on her face.

On the other end of the line, Preston Tilford III sat on the floor of his room, the telephone receiver propped comfortably against his shoulder. He was rereading the letter he had just received from Blake Norton. He smiled a small, indulgent smile. Blake's letters were always terrific, so full of life and vitality, with scribbles and exclamation points and doodles strewn haphazardly all over the page. Just like Blake herself. Of all the girls he had known in his life, only Blake and Mary Ellen Kirkwood had that electric energy, that drive and ambition that he admired so much. If he ever fell in love with anybody in a really serious way (Pres had fallen in love more times than he could count, in a *semiserious* way) it was going to be with a girl with exactly that kind of sparkling energy and drive and ambition — and beauty.

At the thought of Mary Ellen, his mouth quirked a little at one corner and his eyes were drawn to the photograph of the cheerleading squad that stood on his desk. There was Mary Ellen, kneeling beside him on the gym floor, her face close to his, both arms looped around his shoulders, smiling at the photographer — the photographer who just happened to be her boyfriend, Patrick Henley, of course. It was funny, actually. Under other circumstances, he could get really interested in Mary Ellen. In fact, now that he thought about it, he remembered that he *had* been, at one point, or maybe at more than one point. But somehow things just hadn't worked out between them, mainly because Pres had always had the sneaking suspicion that Mary Ellen's interest in him had to do more with his money than anything else. And then Patrick had come along and sort of swept Mary Ellen off her feet — even though she usually tried to act pretty aloof around him and pretend that she wasn't at all interested. But Pres knew better. He had happened on the two of them just today, in fact, standing really close together in front of Mary

7

Ellen's locker, Patrick's arms around Mary Ellen, his lips against her neck. Pres could tell from the dreamy, faraway looks on their faces *exactly* what they were feeling. He knew. He'd felt that way before, too, when he was involved with somebody extra special.

Pres sighed. Sometimes, in spite of all the Tilford money and the vast number of exciting things he found to do with it, he felt lonely, especially when he was between girls. It would be wonderful to be dating somebody like Mary Ellen — beautiful and warm and energetic. In fact, he considered, maybe it would even be nice to date Mary Ellen. In a lot of ways, she was just like him: never satisfied with what she had, always wanting more, always wanting the best for herself. He had to admire that kind of spirit, even if it did seem pretty selfish most of the time. He knew about selfishness, he reminded himself. That was another way that he and Mary Ellen were alike.

Pres sighed again and pulled his eyes away from the picture. Unfortunately, getting together with Mary Ellen was completely out of the question — especially since he had gone into the moving business with Patrick. Pres might be a little unconventional sometimes, but he always respected other people's territory. And Mary Ellen was definitely in Patrick's territory, whether she wanted to admit it or not.

Thinking of Patrick made Pres think about the moving business — and *that* made him think about what was on his mind the most these days. His future. Time was getting short. Graduation would be here in only a few months, and he *had* to come to some decision very soon about what to do next year. Should he stay in Tarenton and help Patrick run the business they had started on a shoestring a few months ago? It was a great temptation. In fact, Pres had been thinking lately, owning a moving company was exactly what he wanted to do for the next couple of years. The idea of having his own business gave him a sense of power and excitement that he had never felt before. Sure, he was a Tilford, and that meant money and power. But it wasn't *his* money or *his* power. It all belonged to Preston Tilford II, and his father never let him forget it.

On the other hand, owning a moving company was exactly what Preston Tilford II *didn't* want him to do — at least, not just now. "I don't have anything against entrepreneurs," his father had said sternly at dinner the night before, as he settled into one of his endless lectures. "In fact, if I weren't an entrepreneur myself, Tarenton Fabricators would never be expanding into new computer-related markets, the way it is today. I have no objections, Pres, to seeing you start a business right here in Tarenton. None at all." He paused and stared over his glasses at Pres for effect, the way he did at board meetings. "But first things first, young man. And the first thing for a Tilford has to be Princeton — *before* he goes into business for himself."

"I know, I know," Pres had answered sulkily. "The first thing for a Tilford is Princeton." It was something he'd been hearing for years.

But the truth of the matter was that he didn't know whether he wanted to go to Princeton or not. He was really undecided. And his indecision, unfortunately, was affecting everything else in his life — his schoolwork, his family life, his relations with his friends, even cheerleading. In fact, Ardith Engborg had read him the riot act just a couple of days before, telling him that if he didn't wake up and pay more attention to his cheerleading routines, she was going to have to take some serious action. She had grinned and Pres had grinned, but he had to agree with Ardith that he wasn't really doing his job. It was hard to concentrate on the present when the future was so uncertain.

"Well, it's about time," Pres grumbled, when Mary Ellen finally came to the phone. "What kept you so long?"

"Really, I'm sorry, Pres," Mary Ellen said contritely. "I was sorting photographs for my portfolio, and I stopped to put them away."

"Yeah, well, speaking of your portfolio, I just got this letter from Blake."

"What's Blake's letter got to do with my portfolio?" Mary Ellen asked.

"She says for you to send it to her," Pres said, glancing at the letter. "She's discovered a modeling outfit in New York that she thinks is just right for you, and she wants to give them your stuff. She thinks they might be interested."

"Oh, Pres, that's wonderful!" Mary Ellen squealed. Pres smiled and held the receiver an inch away from his ear. When Mary Ellen was happy, the whole world knew it. Then there was a brief silence, and Pres put the phone back against his ear. "Except that I just can't send her the portfolio I've got," she added, in a glum voice. "It . . . it's too high-schoolish, full of pictures of cheerleading and school dances and stuff like that. It's really amateurish, Pres. I mean, the pictures are nice, and I'm grateful to Patrick for taking them, but it's like a kid's scrapbook or something. Nobody in New York is going to look at it twice."

Pres heard the despair in Mary Ellen's voice. He could understand and sympathize with the way she felt. She had so much ambition, so much drive to succeed, and she obviously felt awfully limited here in Tarenton. She needed some help. "You know, Mary Ellen," Pres said, thinking out loud, "what *you* need is somebody who could give you some advice about this business. I mean, some *inside* advice."

"Isn't that funny," Mary Ellen replied slowly. "You must be reading my mind, Pres. That's exactly what I was saying to myself just a few minutes ago, while I was looking at these photographs. I need to talk to somebody who knows something about the business." She paused. "But that's impossible here in Tarenton," she added, sounding discouraged. "Absolutely impossible."

"Well, I don't know about that," Pres said. He thought for a minute. "Listen, Mary Ellen, I've got an idea. My father was talking last night at dinner about this new public relations firm he's

11

hired. They're just getting started here in Tarenton, and the guy who owns it is from Chicago. I mean, public relations has got something to do with modeling, doesn't it? Anyway, maybe they'd be able to give you some advice about how to set up your portfolio, or put you in touch with somebody who could help, or — "

"Oh, do you think so, Pres?" Mary Ellen's voice, so discouraged a moment before, sounded as if it might bubble over with sheer happiness. "Actually, all I need is just a little push in the right direction — and some new photographs for my portfolio and suggestions for clothes and — " She stopped. "But I don't know how much I can afford to pay," she said cautiously. "I mean, I still have that money that I inherited a couple of months ago, but. . . ."

"Oh, I think they'll help if I ask them," Pres said, shrugging. "After all, they're working for my dad — and what's the use of being a Tilford if you can't pull a string or two? But listen, Mary Ellen, you shouldn't get your hopes up. I don't know what kind of ideas we'll get out of this guy. Maybe not much."

He paused. With all the worry about his own future, it was kind of crazy to be taking responsibility for Mary Ellen's future. But, then, he had always liked Mary Ellen in a kind of special way, now that he thought about it. The way he felt about her was certainly different from the way he felt about the other cheeleaders, Angie or Nancy or Olivia. It really was too bad she was in Patrick's territory. Since he and Claudia had broken up, he was getting a little tired of spending weekend nights hanging out in front of the television, or going to parties and to the movies by himself. "Listen, I'll get the phone number from Dad and we'll give it a shot," he added. "No guarantees, but we can try. Okay?"

"Okay!" Mary Ellen said enthusiastically. "And . . . and thanks, Pres. You're a lifesaver!" She paused, and her voice grew softer. "Really, I mean it, Pres. You're wonderful."

"Sure," Pres agreed casually. "That's what they all say."

"Yes, but . . . but I really *mean* it, Pres." To Pres's surprise, she sounded as if she did.

"Well, thanks, Mary Ellen," Pres said. "Listen, what would you say if I asked. . . ." But his voice trailed off and he didn't finish the sentence.

"What?" Mary Ellen asked.

"Oh, nothing," Pres answered. "Just daydreaming, I guess." After he put down the phone, he stared at it thoughtfully for a few minutes. It really *was* too bad that Mary Ellen was in Patrick's territory.

CHAPTER

All the other cheerleaders had already gone to the showers, but Olivia Evans and Walt Manners were still in the gym, grimly going over the same series of moves for the third time. "Come on, Walt," Olivia said, after they had messed it up once again. Her voice, taut with frustration, echoed through the empty gym. "This stupid little routine is too simple to keep fouling up like this. Let's get it right, for a change!"

Walt reached for the towel and mopped his round face. His stocky body was soaked with sweat and his T-shirt stuck to his chest. Walt wasn't exactly good-looking, but he was an outstanding gymnast, able to execute complicated movement patterns with an ease and grace that always made them look simple. Walt shook his head. He couldn't understand it. Little four-step routines like this one were always easy for him, and yet here he was, making one ridiculous error after another.

He draped the towel around his neck. "I guess it's my timing," he said, avoiding Olivia's eyes.

"Right," Olivia said sarcastically, watching him. She put her hands on her hips. "It must be your timing," she mocked. "Have you checked your watch lately? Judging from the way you executed that flip, I'd say you're about three minutes and thirty seconds slow."

Walt sat down on a stack of gym mats and looked at Olivia. In spite of his frustration, he couldn't help smiling. No matter how often he was around her, he had to marvel at her pert litheness, her quickness. She was tiny and fragile-looking — like a child, really. Sometimes she looked like a little lost waif, with those big eyes and that slight body. But tucked inside that slender self was an iron will that just wouldn't quit, no matter how long it took to get things right. Walt smiled again. Even though things had always been light and easy and casual between them, it was getting to the point these days where he found himself saying, "I love you" — and meaning it.

And that, without a doubt, Walt knew, was what was throwing his timing off. Loving Olivia. Oh, there was nothing especially wrong with loving Olivia, particularly when you considered what a terrific person she was. But loving Olivia certainly wasn't making his life any easier. For one thing, he'd decided a long time ago that he was going to go to State to major in broadcast journalism. He was good at that sort of thing and that was exactly what he wanted to do with his life. But going to the university would mean leaving Tarenton — and leaving Olivia, who wouldn't be going to college for another year. They were so close that it was hard to even imagine being apart from her.

And now, to complicate matters even further, there was a new opportunity, with his parents, in New York. The Mannerses' agent was suggesting that the three of them — his mother, his father, and Walt — syndicate a television series, an early-morning family talk show that would feature teenagers and adults discussing issues like family conflicts and sex and growing up. What a great opportunity! But they would have to move to New York to do the show, and he would have to postpone his plans for college, and. . . . Walt shook his head, still watching Olivia. He would feel better if he could talk to her about it, but somehow it didn't seem fair, burdening her with all this unsettling stuff when she had things of her own to think about. But not talking about it seemed to make it even worse. It was funny. The future was like a tangled plate of spaghetti. You never could pull out just one single strand. You had to deal with the entire thing, untwist it all at once. No wonder his timing was off.

"What are you staring at?" Olivia asked irritably, pulling on a pair of baggy gray sweat pants. "Listen, Walt, I've had enough. I'm quitting for the day. I can see that you're completely out of it."

"I'm staring at you because you're so cute," Walt retorted with a crooked grin. "Even when you're hacking me into bite-sized pieces with your saber-toothed wit."

Olivia didn't smile back the way she usually did. "I wouldn't have to hack you into pieces, bite-sized or otherwise, if you'd just start paying attention to what's going on around you." She tied the waist string of her sweat pants. "Actually, what you need is a return-trip ticket from whatever foreign country you're visiting in your head." Her mouth was a tight line. "And I'm not the only one who thinks so. Everybody on the squad is asking when you're coming back to join the rest of us."

Walt's grin faded and a red flush rose along his jaw. "Well, I've got a lot on my mind," he muttered. Normally he had a fierce concentration that enabled him to execute his cheerleading routines flawlessly. But lately . . . well, lately, he just hadn't been able to concentrate, and he wasn't surprised that the others had noticed. Ardith Engborg had noticed, too. He had seen her watching him closely this afternoon. He expected that tomorrow she would call him aside and ask him what was on his mind, as she had done a week or so ago. "Just a whole lot on my mind," he repeated defensively, wiping his face again.

"Yeah. So I see." Olivia picked up her towel and headed toward the girls' locker room. "Well, if you can clear your mind, do you think you might be able to give me a ride home in about twenty minutes?" She turned and flashed a teasing smile that lit up her dark eyes. "That is, if you can remember where you parked the Jeep." She walked out without another word, leaving Walt still sitting on the mats, staring after her and smiling, shaking his head.

Olivia had thought that the locker room would be empty, but Nancy Goldstein was still there, standing in front of the mirror, combing her hair, a look of intense excitement on her face. She didn't even seem to notice Olivia when she came in, sat down on the bench, and began to pull off her tennis shoes.

Nancy was tall and dramatic-looking, with dark hair. With her high cheekbones and exotic eyes, she was the sexiest-looking one of the cheerleaders, Olivia had always thought. Now, glancing down at her nearly boyish-looking self and then looking back at Nancy's gorgeous figure, Olivia couldn't help but feel a pang of jealousy. Nancy had the kind of curves that every girl just had to covet.

But Olivia's envy was immediately wiped away when she thought about the past few months. Nobody really envied Nancy anymore, not since the tragic climbing accident that had killed her boyfriend Ben and nearly killed Olivia and Patrick, too. But Ben's death was in the past now, and Nancy's depression seemed to have disappeared almost completely — probably because of Eric Campbell. Olivia had met Eric only once, at the Tri-State High School Cheerleading Competition at Templeton College, but she remembered him as the dark-haired, good-looking guy who had impulsively pulled Nancy to him and kissed her in the wild few minutes after the Tarenton victory. Since then, Nancy and Eric had been going out together regularly, and all Nancy's friends were very much relieved that Nancy's depression was over.

"Ah-hem," Olivia said, clearing her throat.

Nancy jumped and smeared mascara on her cheek with the little blue brush she held in her hand. "Gosh, you startled me, Olivia," she said, wiping off the streak of mascara. "I thought you and Walt were still going over that routine."

"We were," Olivia said darkly, tossing down her shoe in disgust. "Going over it and over it and over it. But when Walt loses his concentration, he can't even see his feet. He just falls apart completely. I finally decided that there just wasn't any point in working on it any longer."

Nancy looked somber. "Well, none of us covered ourselves with glory today, to tell the truth. Ardith was really ticked off about it. She talked to me about it after practice. She thinks everybody's tired of each other and tired of cheerleading. The problem is, there's still plenty left to do this year."

Olivia nodded. "What's *wrong* with everybody these days?" she asked plaintively. "Walt's mind is somewhere over the rainbow, Mary Ellen is completely spaced out, Pres hardly ever speaks

19

to anybody, and Angie is lost in the fog some-place. Our routines are falling apart and Ardith looks like she's going out of her mind trying to figure it all out." She laughed a little. "Has every-body gotten a case of the plague? You and I seem to be the only normal ones left."

Nancy smiled into the mirror, putting her lip-stick on carefully. "Well, don't bet on me," she said. "I'm not feeling very normal these days, with Eric around. I sort of feel sky-high, and getting higher by the minute." She turned around to face Olivia. "Actually, I suppose everybody's got a case of the Senior Blues. It's bound to hap-pen, don't you think? I mean, it's only a couple of months until graduation, and — "

Olivia dropped her other tennis shoe with a thud. "Well, if that's the problem, it lets me out," she said flatly. She was the only one of the cheerleaders who wouldn't be graduating in June, since she was a junior. She looked at Nancy, who was wearing a new green sweater and skirt and a pair of high-heeled suede boots. "You look ter-rific. Are you on your way somewhere special?"

Nancy smiled and put the cap on her lipstick. "Yes. Eric is coaching a swim meet tonight at Hillsborough. And then the team is going to meet at Greg Conners's house for a party afterward. It'll be fun."

Olivia stood up and peeled off her workout suit. "That's great. But I hope that whatever you do, you don't go getting all spacey, like the rest," she said vehemently. "I don't know *what* would happen to the squad if you fell apart, too."

Shivering against the chill, she wrapped herself in a big terry towel. "I guess I'd have to quit and Ardith would probably get fired. And Vanessa Barlow would get the chance she's been waiting for, to organize a substitute cheerleading squad."

Nancy's smile faded and she came over to sit on the bench opposite Olivia. "Oh, it's not that bad," she said. "Vanessa is just going to have to wait." She looked at Olivia thoughtfully. "Listen, Olivia, I wish you'd find it in your heart to have a little sympathy for the rest of us. The pressures of senior year are pretty tough. You know, most of us are trying to figure out what we're going to be doing for the entire rest of our lives. I mean, that's awfully important. And it takes a lot of thought."

Olivia regarded her, remembering how Walt had been avoiding her questions about whether or not he was applying to State. It was something that was bothering him, but he obviously didn't want to talk about it — to her, anyway. "Yes, I guess you're right," she said, after a minute. "I guess you guys have got a lot on your minds. I hadn't thought about it that way."

"Well, it's a real problem," Nancy said, putting her makeup into her purse. "Take me, for instance. I mean, I was pretty well decided on taking that scholarship that State offered me and getting my certificate so that I could teach. But State is two hundred miles away, and if I do that, it'll mean that Eric and I only see each other a couple of times a month." She closed her eyes briefly, remembering the conversation the two of

21

them had had the night before. Eric had tried to talk her into doing the first two years of her college work at Hillsborough, so they could be together. But Hillsborough didn't have the program she wanted. She sighed. It *was* a problem. She turned to Olivia again. "I really don't think I could hold on to Eric if we didn't see each other more often than that. I'm sure he would find another girl friend, somebody he could be with more often."

"Oh really, Nancy, you can't let *Eric* decide your entire future for you!" Olivia exploded. "You've only known him for a little while! I mean, you've got to make your own decision — without letting anybody else influence what you want to do."

Nancy stood up. "Sure. Well, try telling that to Walt," she said quietly, closing her purse and slinging it over her shoulder. "Haven't you figured it out yet? Walt's got the same problem I have. That's exactly what's wrong with his timing."

Olivia stared at her. "Do you think so?"

"Why don't you ask him?" Nancy replied.

"Well, I guess Nancy's right," Walt said, shifting down into second gear as the Jeep climbed the hill to Olivia's house. He was wearing his heavy coat and his favorite plaid hunting cap, with the earflaps tied up on top of his head like a deer hunter. "I guess we're all a little preoccupied these days, trying to figure out what's ahead."

"Well, why would you keep something like that to yourself?" Olivia demanded. "I mean, why didn't you say something about it?"

"I did," Walt said. He pulled to a stop in front of Olivia's house. At one of the front windows, the lace curtain twitched and they could see Olivia's mother watching them out the window. "I mean, I mentioned it. But I didn't want to make a big deal about it."

Olivia sighed. "I wish she'd stop doing that," she said, watching the window. She began to laugh. "Really, I love my mother, but sometimes I wonder about her sanity. What in the world does she think we can do, anyway, sitting here in this wide-open Jeep in thirty-degree weather, in broad daylight, right in front of everybody who happens to drive past?"

Walt turned toward her. "Well, we might try doing this, for starters," he said promptly, and pulled her against him. Surprised, Olivia struggled for an instant, but then she forgot where they were and yielded to the urgency of Walt's kiss.

"My goodness," Olivia said, after a few minutes, when they had pulled apart. At the front window, the curtain was twitching excitedly. Olivia felt breathless. "A few kissing lessons certainly have gone a long way, haven't they?" Only a month before, they had been joking about Walt's abrupt style of kissing. "More like smashing than smooching," Olivia had called it, and they had spent a lot of time practicing. She laughed. "We're really getting to be experts."

"I don't think it's the kissing lessons that are doing it," Walt said soberly. He was staring at Olivia, his eyes dark. "At least as far as I'm concerned. I think . . . I think it's the idea of maybe having to go away next year, to college or wherever, and not seeing you for a while. It makes me think."

Olivia looked down and twisted her wool scarf. "Yes, I know," she said, trying to steady her voice after Walt's kiss. She had always been one to look on the practical side of things, and even though it was painful to think of Walt a couple of hundred miles away, she knew that going to the university was the best thing for him. "But even if it hurts, we can't let the future get in the way of the present. Or the present get in the way of the future," she added thoughtfully, remembering what she had told Nancy. "And anyway, State isn't that far away. We can see each other pretty often, can't we?"

Walt sighed and put both hands on the steering wheel, thinking about New York. The city was more than a couple of hundred miles away, and if they decided to do the television show, it would mean he could see Olivia only every couple of months. But he didn't want to talk to her about *that* until there was something more definite. So he just said, with a little lopsided grin, "I wish you wouldn't always be so practical, Olivia. Don't you have any romance in your soul?"

"Well, one of us has to be practical," Olivia responded tartly. "And I've got a *lot* of romance in my soul, when the temperature isn't thirty degrees and dropping." She glanced toward the window. For the moment, the curtain was quiet, and she turned toward Walt, putting her hand on his shoulder and brushing his cheek with her mittened fingers. "Listen, Walt, you're the one who has to decide what you want for yourself. You can't design your future with me in mind. That's just not fair to you." She looked at him again. "I don't mean that I don't care for you," she whispered. "I just mean. . . ." She couldn't finish the sentence.

"You're right," Walt said. He seized her hand and pulled her toward him again. "Hey, your mom's getting bored, sitting at that window all by herself. Let's give her some more excitement."

So they did.

CHAPTER

"Grrr," Angie Poletti said fiercely. She scowled and tossed her long, honey-colored hair as she helped herself to cottage cheese. Angie was on one of her perennial diets, and being on a diet sometimes made her act edgy and out of sorts.

Olivia laughed. "You, too?" she asked. She added another heaping spoonful of macaroni salad to her plate. Olivia was surprised to see Angie so upset. Of all the cheerleaders, she was the one who was usually the sweetest and most even-tempered, the one who could take everything, no matter how nerve-wracking, in her stride.

"What do you mean, 'You, too'?" Angie demanded crossly, reaching across a tempting bowl of salad dressing for a carrot. "All I said was that I wished Mary Ellen would stop pushing everybody around. Sometimes she acts like she has property rights to everybody's ideas. Really, she's getting to be a major pain." She glared at the carrot.

"I know," Olivia said wryly. "I heard you." She laughed again.

Angie regarded Olivia with suspicion as they went through the cash-register checkout. "Honestly, Olivia, I don't know what you're finding to laugh about. Mary Ellen's behavior isn't at all funny. If you ask me, it's pretty rotten."

"I'm laughing to keep from crying, if you want to know the truth," Olivia said grimly. She looked over the crowded cafeteria. Usually, she and Walt ate lunch together, but he had flown to New York with his parents for a few days on some sort of mysterious and important errand that he wouldn't tell her about. So today she was eating with Angie.

"What's the matter? Are you lonesome for Walt already?" Following after Olivia, Angie put her tray on the table beside the window. "He's only been gone a day or so, for heaven's sake. Isn't he coming back tomorrow?"

"It's not Walt I'm thinking about," Olivia said slowly, pulling out her chair. It would be good to talk to Angie about what was happening, she decided. She had Nancy's opinion, but sometimes Nancy didn't see things the way they really were. Angie, on the other hand, usually had her head on straight about people and the way they related to one another. Olivia sat down, looking across the table at Angie. "Angie, why do I have this

27

awful feeling that there's something really *wrong* with the cheerleading squad?"

Angie looked at her, one eyebrow raised. "Maybe because it's true," she said calmly.

"You mean you've noticed it, too? It's not just my imagination?"

Angie didn't answer right away. And when she spoke, she only said, "Why don't you tell me what *you've* noticed."

Olivia buttered her roll. "Well, for starters, I'd say that for the last few weeks everybody's been getting on everybody else's nerves, in a big way. You're mad at Mary Ellen for acting so pushy. Nancy's not speaking to Pres because he forgot to set up the practice mats a couple of days ago. Pres is ticked off at Walt for messing up the handstand routine the other night, and Walt has it in for Nancy for ducking out of practice last week. And worst of all, Ardith is absolutely furious with all of us." Olivia opened her milk carton and inserted her straw. "What's going on? I mean, we're all acting like a bunch of crazy little kids. Loony tunes. Everything's going to pieces."

Angie shrugged. "Well, maybe we've all got other things on our minds," she said. To Olivia, her tone sounded defensive — which was strange, because Angie was *never* defensive. "Is that so bizarre?"

"Other things?" Olivia asked. "*What* other things? Sure, everybody's busy with school and stuff like that. But cheerleading is supposed to be our highest extracurricular priority, isn't it? And what's going to happen to the squad if we

28

keep on chewing each other into little pieces the way we're doing?"

"Oh, come on, Olivia," Angie said, taking the top off her orange juice bottle and pouring the juice into a glass. There was a tone of sharp irritation in her voice, and Olivia looked up at her in surprise. Angie *never* sounded this irritated, even when she was on her strictest diet. "Nobody's going to do anything that will *really* hurt the squad," she was saying. "All of us love cheerleading too much for that, and we have too much respect for Ardith. But the simple fact is that right now most of us have other things to think about besides Varsity Cheerleading. I mean, really important things."

"Yeah? Like what kind of important things?"

"Well, important things like what we're going to do next year, for example," Angie said. She looked down at her cottage cheese and wrinkled her nose distastefully. "For me, it's a big question. Maybe the biggest question of my life."

Olivia groaned. So Nancy had been right. "So *that's* what this is all about."

"Well, of course it is," Angie said. She picked up her fork. "I mean, Chris and I have been talking about nothing but this college thing for the last couple of weeks." She took a deep, unsteady breath. "I've already submitted my application to State and it looks like I might even get a scholarship there. Chris would like to go to State with me, but his father is dead set on his going to Yale, the way *he* did." She looked downcast and began to poke listlessly at her cottage cheese with her fork. "I mean, it doesn't seem very fair. Chris and I have just found one another and now. . . ."

Olivia nodded sympathetically. Chris was a transfer student at Tarenton and one of the best-looking boys in the senior class. Angie, even though she was pretty and smart and athletic and really sweet, had always seemed to be everybody's friend and nobody's girl friend. It had taken a long time for her to believe that Chris could actually be in love with her, the way he claimed to be. But when he had finally managed to convince her, Angie couldn't hide her feelings. She was in love — no doubt about it.

"I know," Olivia said thoughtfully. "I guess Walt and I have the same problem — about next year, I mean. But I'm not too worried about it. I can't help believing that we'll work it out somehow. State is only a couple of hundred miles away." She patted Angie's hand comfortingly. "You and Chris will work it out, too."

"That's easy for *you* to say, Olivia," Angie objected. Olivia pulled her hand back. "For one thing, you're a junior. You still have another year here at Tarenton, so you don't have all the uncertainty of figuring out what *you* want to do with your future. And for another thing, you and Walt have been dating for quite a while, and you're settled. I mean, both of you know what you want, and you're sure about the way you feel about one another. Even if Walt goes away to school, you know you'll still manage to be together, one way or another. But Chris and I are just getting started, and if he goes to one school and I go to another . . . well, I just have this awful feeling that we're going to break up and there's nothing I can do about it."

Olivia shook her head sadly. If Angie was feeling so low and insecure about such an important part of her life, did that mean that everybody else was, too? "Do you think *everybody* is bothered by pretty much the same thing?" she asked. "Pres and Mary Ellen and Nancy, too? Is that why the squad is falling apart?"

"I don't *think*," Angie replied. "I *know*. Just yesterday, Pres was telling me that his dad is putting a lot of pressure on him to go to Princeton, when what he really wants to do is — "

"Well, hello there, little munchkins," a cool, brittle voice said. Olivia looked up. It was Vanessa Barlow, balancing her lunch tray against one hip. She was wearing a pair of tight leather jeans and a long, lean black sweater. "You two look as if you're mourning the sudden passing of a very dear friend. Who's dead?" Vanessa's short dark hair was brushed forward into spikes all around her face and she was wearing a great deal of blue eye makeup, with dusky circles around her eyes. Olivia stifled a giggle. She thought Vanessa's hair and makeup made her look more like a witch than ever.

"Hello, Vanessa," Angie said, looking up and smiling. Angie was everybody's friend, the only one of the cheerleaders who even pretended to tolerate Vanessa. "Nobody's dead, actually. Or at least not yet. We were just talking about next

31

year. About life after graduation — if there *is* such a thing."

"Of course there's life after graduation," Vanessa said. Her smile had a self-satisfied look to it. "As a matter of fact, I've just had some absolutely *stunning* news about next year. It looks as if I'm all set."

Olivia made a little face into her milk carton. When Vanessa came along, the conversation always took a sudden, sharp turn — in Vanessa's exclusive direction.

"What are you going to do?" Angie asked.

Vanessa looked triumphant. "I've just won a scholarship to the Madison School of Design, in Chicago," she purred. "It's an extremely competitive school. They're so exclusive that they accept only a few of the very best students every year." She glanced at Olivia. "Of course, you've heard of it."

"No, actually, I haven't," Olivia said. "As a matter of fact," she added innocently, "I thought you were going to Vassar. I was sure that you had already applied, and you were certain you would get in." She turned to Angie. "Didn't you think Van was going to Vassar, Angie? Why, didn't we hear her talk about planning to see the Vassar admissions counselor?"

Angie spluttered in her orange juice. Some of the girls had turned the tables on Vanessa a while back, making her think that her interview with the Vassar admissions counselor would go much more smoothly if it was greased with the offer of a little cash. Her application to the college had been turned down on the spot.

Vanessa flushed, shifted her tray from one hip to the other, looking angry. "Who wants to go to a dinky little school out in the middle of nowhere?" she asked, tossing her head carelessly. "Poughkeepsie, phooey. I'd *much* rather be in Chicago, where there's plenty of excitement. And Madison is a wonderful place to study design."

"I didn't know you were interested in design," Angie remarked. "What kind of design?"

"Well, it all happened rather suddenly," Vanessa replied evasively. "And design isn't the only thing I'll be studying there. I'm also interested in writing. Professionally, that is." Her smile seemed to have a knowing edge. "In fact, I've been asked to do a special assignment for our school paper. They've made me a feature writer, you know." She waited to see the impact of her words.

Olivia gave an inward grimace. Feature writer! Now Vanessa would have another way to spread her poison. She stifled a giggle. Poison pen.

Tired of waiting, Vanessa turned to go. "Well, I'm sure you'll be hearing more about that before too long," she said. "In the meantime, I certainly do hope that both of you manage to get your troubles ironed out. It's such a *terrible* nuisance to look so pale and washed-out because you're feeling draggy and way below par, isn't it?" She leaned confidentially toward the girls. "Really, you should both relax and stop worry-

33

ing so much about things. It's doing horrible things to your complexions." With that, she turned and left.

Olivia and Angie sat silent for a minute, staring open-mouthed at Vanessa's departing back as she swayed toward another table. "Do I look pale and washed-out?" Angie asked finally.

"No," Olivia said. "Is there something the matter with my complexion?"

"No," Angie replied, frowning. "Your complexion is fine. Just fine." She looked once again after Vanessa. "Grrr," she said. "Toxic. That's the only word for Vanessa. Just plain toxic."

Olivia laughed, thinking about poison pens, and after a moment, Angie joined in.

At the other end of the cafeteria, Pres was just sitting down at a table next to Mary Ellen. "Do you know where Patrick is?" he asked, putting his arm across the back of her chair. He noticed that Mary Ellen looked exceptionally pretty today. Her blonde hair was pulled back in a sleek ponytail, and she was wearing a blue sweater that brought out the cornflower-blue color of her eyes. Just looking at her made Pres feel good. "I need to talk to him about a moving job we've got this weekend," he added. "Mr. Howard wants us to move some equipment from his garage to his shop across town."

Mary Ellen looked a little cross. In fact, thinking about Patrick Henley was almost a guarantee that she would feel somewhat cross. "No," she said firmly, "I do not know where Patrick Henley is." She pushed her tray away and folded her arms on the table. Pres looked unusually handsome today, in a striped shirt and a gray cashmere pullover sweater, and she could detect the lingering scent of an expensive cologne. To her surprise, she felt a faint tingling across the back of her neck and a warm, melting feeling somewhere inside her. A new thought came into her mind. Was it possible that she was beginning to be attracted — physically attracted — to Pres? She had been attracted to him in other ways, before — after all, he had the kind of money and power that she wanted. But this felt different. This felt more . . . well, more physical, somehow. It was an intriguing idea, an idea worth testing.

She leaned toward him and smiled a soft, half-teasing smile. "After all, why should I know where Patrick Henley is? I mean, he and I aren't anything terribly special to each other." For a second, the words stabbed her painfully. They weren't *really* true. She knew that she was special to Patrick and, in spite of her best intentions, he was special to her. But that wasn't the way she *wanted* it to be, was it? What she wanted, more than anything else in the world, was to stop being poor, stop having to count every nickel twice. And Patrick Henley, sweet and handsome and very, very sexy as he was, was simply not the person to help her reach her goal. But Pres might be. He just might be. "Really, Pres," she added softly and with a little sparkle in her eyes, "haven't you known me long enough to realize that I couldn't *really* be committed to a garbage man?"

Pres moved a little closer. Mary Ellen's eyes were almost hypnotic, and when she looked down, her thick, full lashes brushed her cheek softly. Why hadn't he ever noticed how thick her lashes were, how blue her eyes were? There had been a time before when he was attracted to her, but he'd felt that she might have been manipulating him, using him to get the power that she wanted. But right now, he didn't feel that way at all — and anyway, if she was, what did it matter? He used people that way, too, didn't he? He and Mary Ellen were *very* much alike, and that made the attraction just that much stronger.

"Listen, if I *really* thought that were true, Mary Ellen. . . ." His voice trailed off. Was he imagining it, or was there something very different in the way Mary Ellen was looking at him? Suddenly the din of the cafeteria seemed to fade into the background and he was conscious only of the two of them, sitting close together, a kind of electrical current lighting up the space between them.

"It's true, Pres," Mary Ellen said.

But then he suddenly thought about Patrick and the thought was like a splash of cold water, bringing him back to the immediate present with a shiver. He might be enormously attracted to Mary Ellen, but there was still his friend to consider. "Well, maybe it's true for you," he said. "But I can tell by the way that Patrick looks at you that he — "

"Listen, Pres, I'm not responsible for the way Patrick Henley looks at me," Mary Ellen interrupted intently. She leaned back in her chair and Pres could feel the warmth of her shoulder against his fingers. The feeling traveled up his arm, making it a little hard to concentrate on Mary Ellen's words. He could only concentrate on the way her lips moved. ". . . and in fact," she was saying, when Pres came back to the present, "I've told him dozens of times that I can't be serious about him."

Pres leaned forward. His fingers longed to find their way to the back of Mary Ellen's bare neck, under her ponytail, where it looked sweet and vulnerable. "Is that really true, Mary Ellen?" he asked, in a low voice. "I mean, I like Patrick a lot, and I wouldn't want to do anything to endanger our partnership — or our friendship."

"Neither would I," Mary Ellen said flatly. There was an odd twist to her mouth, but she was smiling, anyway. "I like him a lot and I want him to be happy, Pres. But being happy isn't going to include me."

Pres smiled. He still wasn't sure about Patrick, but he *was* sure about one thing: He wanted to be with Mary Ellen Kirkwood. He wanted to be with her tonight, and tomorrow night, and. . . . "Well, if that's the case," he said, sitting up straight, "how about going over to the Pizza Palace with me this afternoon after cheerleading practice?"

Mary Ellen nodded happily. "I'd love to." At that moment, the bell rang for the next period and she stood and picked up her tray. "By the way, have you had time to talk to that PR person you mentioned on the phone the other night?" she added, as a casual afterthought. "You know, the guy who's working for your dad?"

"Oh, yeah," Pres said. "I meant to tell you, but I . . . I got sidetracked." Some sidetrack, he thought. His fingers were still tingling where they had brushed against Mary Ellen's shoulder. "His name is Paul Howell. I met him at Dad's office yesterday and mentioned our idea to him. He said he'd be glad to give you some advice if he could, although he's not sure what you want. Turns out he's got a sister who's done some modeling out on the West Coast."

Mary Ellen turned a radiant face toward him. "Really? Oh, Pres, that's wonderful! I . . . I can't thank you enough!" Impulsively, she stood on tiptoe to kiss his cheek. "Listen, I have to go to class. I'll see you at practice, okay?"

"Okay," Pres said, and stood watching as she hurried away. His cheek burned where her lips had touched it.

CHAPTER

"Hey, back off, will you?" Pres said disgustedly to Olivia. "Just back off." He turned his chair around and sat down on it, his arms crossed on the back. "I don't want to hear any more about it."

"Come on, you two," Mary Ellen whispered, with a frown at Pres and an angry shake of her head at Olivia. "Cut it out. Olivia, you're acting like a kid. You don't want Ardith to come into the office and hear this kind of juvenile stuff, do you?"

"Mary Ellen, you're the one who's acting like a kid," Walt said in an I'm-only-trying-to-be-reasonable tone of voice. He was leaning against the wall, hands in his pockets. "Olivia was just trying to tell Pres — "

"Nobody needs to stand up for me, Walter Manners," Olivia retorted hotly, her face getting red. "I can stand up for myself, if you don't mind." She turned to Mary Ellen. "Listen, Mary Ellen, what gives you the right — "

"Nothing gives her the right," Angie remarked, from her usual place in the corner of the coach's office. "She just *takes* it, that's all — the way everybody else on this squad seems to be doing these days." Angie threw a meaningful glance at Nancy.

"And what's *that* supposed to mean?" Nancy asked, with an angry tilt of her chin. "If you think you can — "

"Stop! Stop it this minute!"

There was sudden silence. The Varsity Cheerleaders looked up. Ardith Engborg, their coach, was standing in the open doorway, her hands on her hips, her eyes flashing fire. She was short and slight, but standing straight with her shoulders pulled back, she seemed to fill the whole doorway.

"I do not want to hear another word of this ridiculous and unnecessary hostility," Ardith said firmly into the sudden quiet. She went to her desk and sat down on the corner of it. "Nobody is going to war around here — at least, not as long as I've got anything to say about it. So put up your guns."

"But all I said was — " Mary Ellen began, looking uncomfortable.

At the same time, Walt began, "Olivia was only trying to — "

"I said *put up your guns!*" Ardith roared. Mary

Ellen and Walt subsided. Pres yawned widely, covering a grin.

"That goes for you, too, Preston Tilford," Ardith said, swiveling angrily to face him. "Stop grinning." Pres swallowed his grin, looking repentent. She glared at the others. "And as for every single one of you, I don't want to hear another word out of your mouths for at least three minutes. Is that absolutely clear?"

Everyone nodded dumbly.

"All right. Now I'm going to talk and you're going to listen. And we're all going to get something straight." Ardith went around the desk and rocked back in her chair and looked from one to the other. "I am perfectly aware that a deadly epidemic of the Senior Blues has infected the entire cheerleading squad. You are all contagious. I can hear it in the way you talk, and see it in the way you look at one another, in the way you move — and in the way you *don't* move." Olivia giggled nervously and the coach glared at her. "You're only living in the here-and-now for part of the time; the other part of the time you're living in next August or next October or next January. You're thinking about *next year* when you ought to be thinking about *this year*. As far as your cheerleading is concerned, your timing is lousy, your routines are sloppy, and you're losing your edge. But I'm not going to let that continue. Got that? After all, this season isn't over yet. There are more games and more cheerleading activities, and *Tarenton needs a squad!*" She sat up straight and banged her fist on the desk. A pencil holder fell over, but Ardith didn't even notice. "We're going to have a squad, if I have to shut you all in the locker rooms with nothing to eat but oatmeal and water for a solid week until we straighten this thing out!" She glared at them. "Do you understand me?"

A mutter of chastened "Yes, ma'am"'s ran around the room.

Pres sat up straighter. "Listen, Ardith, I just want to say that I'm sorry I haven't been — "

"Say it to Nancy," Ardith said shortly. "She's the one who had to put out the mats when you didn't show up to do your job." She turned to Mary Ellen. "And while Pres is taking care of that little chore, I think you ought to apologize to everybody for being such a tyrant lately."

Mary Ellen looked startled. "Have I been. . . ?" she asked meekly.

"Yes, you have," Ardith said, with firm emphasis.

"Listen, everybody, I'm really sorry," Mary Ellen said, looking around. "I didn't mean. . . ."

"And the rest of you can bury your hatchets right now," Ardith went on. She pulled out the stopwatch that always hung on a chain around her neck. "I'll give you exactly two minutes to get the job done."

Angie turned to Nancy. "I'm sorry," she muttered. "I don't know what got into me. I don't want *anything* to come between us, Nancy."

Nancy hugged her, and Olivia hugged both of them. Walt came up and joined in with the three of them. In the other corner, Pres and Mary Ellen were standing close together, their arms around one another.

After a minute, Pres left Mary Ellen and came over to Nancy. "I'm sorry about the mats," he said. "Honest."

Nancy nodded. "It's okay," she shrugged, with a smile. "A little extra lifting never hurt anybody."

Ardith checked her watch and held up her hand. "Okay, squad, fun time is over," she said. "Does everybody feel better?" Expectantly, she cupped her hand behind her right ear.

"Yes, ma'am," everybody chorused loudly.

"Right," Ardith said, satisfied. "Yes, ma'am. Very good." There was a relaxed grin on her face. "However, I will have to reserve judgment about just how much better you feel until I see how much more smoothly you work." She clasped her hands behind her head and leaned back. "And in the meantime, I have an idea for you to think about." She looked around at all of them. "You don't have to give me your responses to it right now; you can go away and think about it and discuss it among yourselves. We'll talk tomorrow after practice."

Walt regarded her curiously. "What's up?" he asked.

Ardith answered his question with another question. "Have you noticed that we have a very unusual situation this year?" she asked. "Five out of the six of you are seniors. That means that there will be at least five new cheerleaders on

43

next year's squad. Olivia will be the only one who will be available to help the new group get started. And *that* means that next year we'll be starting over, completely, from scratch. It can be done, but it's going to be a tough job."

Olivia squirmed. Of course she had known all along that she was the only junior on the squad, but she hadn't thought of it in terms of what was going to happen next year. Suddenly, the idea of trying out with a whole bunch of new people, with all the other cheerleaders gone, made her feel terribly sad and lonely. She looked around, beginning to feel the enormous pain of the loss that lay ahead. How could she *stand* to have all her friends go away? How could she stand to be the one left behind? Suddenly, she could feel the weight that the others must have been carrying for the last few weeks, and the burden of it made her eyes fill with tears. Walt glanced at her and then quietly took her hand.

Mary Ellen looked around at the others. "You know, I hadn't even thought about what's going to happen to the cheerleading squad next year," she said softly. "Olivia will be the only one of us left. We'll *all* be gone."

Pres whistled between his teeth. "Now that you mention it, Ardith, I can see that you just might have a small problem," he said.

"Correction," Ardith said firmly, glancing at him with an enigmatic smile. "*We* have a problem. You don't think I'm going out there to center court to face this situation all by myself, do you?"

"Well, I don't see what *we* can do," Angie said, with a plaintive look. "After all, we won't be here next fall to help out."

"Maybe not, but you can help me get a head start on next year's squad," Ardith said. "At the same time, you can work on a project that will take your minds off the Senior Blues and get you on the fast track to recovery." She leaned forward and picked up a sheet of paper. "I've been watching the younger students practicing cheers out on the lawn during lunch period and after school." She looked around. "Have you? Been watching them, I mean?"

Mary Ellen twisted uneasily in her chair. "Well, I guess I've noticed that a big bunch of the sophomore and junior girls are doing *something* out there during the lunch hour," she said, with a slight smile. "I mean, they're doing a lot of jumping around and turning cartwheels and stuff, the way we used to, a long time ago." To tell the truth, Mary Ellen really hadn't *wanted* to watch the noisy gang that gathered on the lawn. Some of the group actually looked talented, and it made her feel oddly uncomfortable to think that some of them might be on the next Tarenton Varsity Cheerleading Squad. They would be wearing uniforms exactly like theirs, doing routines very much like theirs, and leading the Tarenton Wolves to new and maybe even more exciting victories. She shivered. It definitely wasn't something she wanted to think about.

"Yes. Well, those kids out there on the lawn have been doing more than just *something*,"

45

Ardith responded dryly, glancing at Mary Ellen. "Some of them are pretty good, if you ask me." With a wicked grin on her face, she jerked her thumb over her shoulder toward the window behind the desk. "I can make that judgment, you see, because this window is very handy. It overlooks the area on the lawn where they have been practicing, even on the coldest days. I've got a bird's-eye view." She laughed. "In fact, I think they practice there on purpose, so that I can't miss them."

"Oh, really?" Pres asked. There was a new interest in his voice. "Well, if you've been keeping an eye on them, you must have an opinion about whether any of them are any good."

"I do," Ardith said. "I do indeed." She surveyed the squad. "My considered opinion is that these students have been watching your routines like beady-eyed hawks. They've been making notes and practicing diligently — and with just a little help and a few pointers, one or two of them could probably step in and replace one or two of you tomorrow."

There was a long, uncomfortable silence, while all the cheerleaders glanced around the room. "Hey, come on, Ardith," Walt said finally, looking concerned. "You've got to be exaggerating. They can't be *that* good." Everybody laughed uneasily.

"Don't laugh, gang," Ardith cautioned, shaking her head. "Go out to the lawn tomorrow and take a look for yourselves. A *long* look. Some of these kids *are* that good. In fact, I genuinely hope that they are. If I'm going to whip together a respectable cheerleading squad in time for the first Tarenton football game next fall, I'm going to have to *count* on their being that good." Her mouth got tight. "In fact, I understand that the school newspaper is interested in doing a feature story about trying out, in order to ensure that there's plenty of interest in the squad for next year."

Olivia sneaked a glance at Angie, wondering if she remembered what Vanessa had said about writing feature stories for the paper. Maybe *that* was what was behind Vanessa's sudden passion for journalism. If it was true, that meant they were all in for a hard time. Vanessa's pen was bound to be as poisonous as her tongue.

"I still don't understand," Nancy was saying with a puzzled frown. "Maybe there *are* a few good cheerleaders coming up. After all, most of us were out there on that lawn every day practicing last year. But I still don't see what any of this has to do with us. I mean, we won't even be around next fall — except for Olivia, that is. How can we help?"

Ardith looked around. "I think we ought to have a clinic."

"A clinic?" Mary Ellen asked doubtfully. "I really don't think any of us have the time to organize — "

"Sure," Pres said, grinning at Ardith. "A *cheerleading* clinic! It's a great idea!"

47

"Yeah. For all the kids who want to try out next year," Walt added, with a meaningful look at Olivia.

"What a *nifty* idea," Angie said, under her breath. There was an unusual note of sarcasm in her voice. "We don't have enough to do now, so we can all — "

"*Stop!*" Ardith said, holding up her hand again. Everybody stopped. "I said I don't want to talk about it now. I want you all to go away and talk about it together and come back and give me your ideas." She stood up. "Tomorrow."

Angie and Nancy pulled on their coats and left together, walking through the gray, chilly twilight into the parking lot. By the time they got to Nancy's car, almost everyone else had gone. Pres's red Porsche was the only other car left in the lot.

"Are you going to study with Chris tonight?" Nancy asked, looking worried as she dug in her purse for her keys. "I hear that tomorrow's calculus test is really going to be tough, and I thought maybe I could join the two of you." She sighed as she unlocked the car door and climbed in. "Calculus is just not at the center of my existence these days, if you want to know the truth. I haven't had time to study for the test and I'm scared I'm going to fail it."

Angie walked around the car and waited for Nancy to unlock the door. "No, we're not studying together," she said quietly, as she settled into the seat and fastened her seat belt. "Chris is working on his Yale application tonight."

"Uh-oh," Nancy said. She turned on the ignition.

"Uh-oh is right."

"Do you think he's actually going to go to Yale? Listening to him talking about it at lunch the other day, I was sure that he'd rather go to State, so the two of you could be together."

Angie shrugged. "Sometimes I wonder whether it's what *he* wants so much as what his *dad* wants that matters." She looked straight ahead, her face set. "I always thought that my senior year was going to be the most wonderful time of my life — and after Chris came along I was sure of it. Now I don't know. It seems like every day I'm less sure . . . of everything." She laughed a little. "Sometimes I don't even know whether or not I've got the energy to get out there on the court and cheer, much less help put on a cheerleading clinic. I wish Ardith hadn't suggested it."

Nancy put the car in gear. "Yes. I know what you mean."

CHAPTER

The Pizza Palace was warm and steamy when Mary Ellen and Pres walked in, shivering from the chilly evening breeze. They found a booth in the corner and gave their orders to the waitress. Mary Ellen sat back with a contented sigh, smiling across the table at Pres. Now, *this* was more like it. She had really felt like somebody special tonight, roaring away from the Tarenton High parking lot in Pres's high-powered red Porsche with genuine sheepskin seat covers and a heater that *really* kept your feet warm. It was just about as far away from Patrick's clunky garbage truck or her parents' miserable old secondhand station wagon as you could get. And when she and Pres had walked into the restaurant together, heads had turned, people had looked at them. Well, why not? Two of Tarenton's popular Varsity Cheerleaders, attractive, lively, full of fun. And

— maybe the best part of all — with Pres, she didn't have to worry whether the two of them had enough money between them to buy a large pizza with the works, or whether they'd have to settle for a medium one, or even a small one with cheese only, the way she and Patrick sometimes had to do. Yes, it felt good to be here with Pres. There was no doubt about it — this was exactly the right thing to do. Why hadn't she considered it before?

"Penny for your thoughts," Pres offered. He grinned. "Or has inflation pushed that up to a quarter?" It was a good question to ask Mary Ellen, he figured. She always knew the value of things.

"Oh." Mary Ellen blushed and looked away. "Oh, I was just thinking . . . about Ardith's idea," she said. "About the cheerleading clinic, I mean."

Hands behind his head, Pres leaned back in the booth and watched Mary Ellen through half-closed eyes. She *was* beautiful, a few honey-colored tendrils escaping from her ponytail, her eyes lowered, a blush staining her cheeks, her mouth soft and half smiling. He'd lay odds that she hadn't *really* been thinking about Ardith's idea. He wondered what she had been thinking about, and the question made him feel, well, hopeful. Funny, he'd never really felt that way about Mary Ellen before, maybe because their cheerleading brought them together so much of the time. Or maybe because he'd always figured that she was only out to get what she wanted: fame, fortune, a rich boyfriend. But somehow, just now, it didn't really matter a whole lot if that's how Mary Ellen felt. What mattered was the way he was feeling about her. He wondered what she would say if he told her what *he* was thinking.

But he only grinned lazily, stretched, and said, "To tell you the truth, I thought Ardith's idea was okay. You were the one who didn't seem to think it was so hot." He paused. "What's the matter, Mary Ellen? Are you worried about what's going to happen when somebody steps into our tennis shoes? I mean, after all, we *are* replaceable. We're not the first cheerleaders that Tarenton has ever had, and we certainly won't be the last."

Mary Ellen made a little face at him. "Yes, I know all that," she said. "I just feel — " She stopped. It was hard to say just how she *did* feel. Of course she knew that she was replaceable as a cheerleader. But it made her uncomfortable to think about somebody else being captain of the squad — somebody who might even be better at the job than she was. But she couldn't really tell Pres that. He'd just laugh and accuse her of being jealous. It would be better to find a different excuse.

"Well," she said finally, "all of us certainly have a lot to do right now. I'm almost a week behind in a couple of my subjects. And none of us has ever been involved with a cheerleading clinic. We don't know the first thing about how to do it. It would be an awful lot of work and — "

Pres held up his hand and Mary Ellen stopped

talking. "But you've got to look at this thing from Ardith's point of view, Mary Ellen," he said persuasively, leaning forward. "I mean, she's got a big problem, it seems to me. And if we can help her figure out whether there's any cheerleading talent buried under all that energetic pop and fizz she's seen, then I think we ought to do it. Even if it takes a weekend or so out of our lives." He laughed and touched her hand. "So what's another weekend or two? We just tear them up and throw them away, anyway."

Mary Ellen couldn't help smiling. "Well, maybe that's what you do with *your* weekends," she said sarcastically. "But don't you think it would take more than a weekend to plan something like this and publicize it and. . . ."

Pres grinned again, liking the spirited way she looked at him. He'd always admired that about her — her spirit. "You can 'Yes, but' all you want, Mary Ellen Kirkwood," he said firmly, "but as far as I'm concerned, I'm going to support Ardith. I think we owe her that much. Don't you?"

"Well, I suppose I do," Mary Ellen said reluctantly. "But think of all the time it's going to take to put this together. And I've got this new portfolio to worry about and. . . ."

At that point the waitress brought their pizza, dripping with cheese and crusted with mushrooms and pepperoni, and the two of them dug in hungrily. After they were finished, Pres leaned back and eyed Mary Ellen. "How about going for a ride around Narrow Brook Lake?" he

53

asked, his voice carefully casual. It was something he'd been thinking about for the last ten minutes.

Mary Ellen looked undecidedly at her watch. "Oh, Pres, I promised Gemma I'd help her with her math homework tonight. . . ." Having a pizza with Pres was one thing, she thought. Going for a ride with him might be something else altogether. It might lead to something that she wasn't sure she was ready for.

"Well, it's no big deal," Pres said casually. "I just thought that it might be a good idea if we talked a little bit about the PR man, Paul Howell, and you let me know when you want to see him."

Mary Ellen nodded slowly. It *was* important to talk about seeing Paul Howell. The sooner she talked to him and found out whether he could help, the sooner she could start making her plans. And there was something else, too, something that had been happening for the last half hour that she had been sitting here with Pres. Inside her again was a warm, melting feeling, and she had the urge to test it, to see if what she felt with Pres was anything like the way she felt with Patrick. If it was, then it might be a sign that she should get serious about Pres.

"Okay," she agreed finally. "You can tell me what kind of a person Mr. Howell is and what you think I ought to tell him about myself." She picked up her purse. "But first let me call Gemma and tell her I'm going to be a little late."

After Mary Ellen had telephoned, the two of

them left the restaurant and headed for the Porsche, parked under a streetlight. It was getting colder, and Pres had slipped his arm companionably around her shoulders, enjoying the way Mary Ellen laughed up at him through the dark.

"Well, isn't this a cozy twosome?" a voice asked coolly, as Pres unlocked the door and opened it for Mary Ellen. "What's our good friend Patrick Henley going to say about it?"

"Isn't it time you took your broom and went home, Vanessa?" Mary Ellen asked, a barb in her voice. There was nothing wrong in having a pizza with Pres, she thought defensively as she slid into the seat, or going for a ride with him either, for that matter. Especially since they had business to discuss. She certainly wasn't going to let Vanessa spoil the evening by reminding her about Patrick. And anyway, even if Patrick knew that she had been out with Pres, what did it matter? They weren't married or anything, for heaven's sake. They weren't even officially going together. She shivered, fighting the anger that boiled up inside her. After all that had happened this year, she had a right to hate Vanessa.

Vanessa, who was bundled up in a black furry jacket, a bright red hat, and red gloves, was just getting out of her parked car. Harry Mathias, one of the Tarenton basketball players, was with her. Pres grinned at Vanessa. It made him feel good to have her see him with Mary Ellen. Van had spirit, too, and he'd always admired her, even when she was being witchy. And it made him feel especially good to see jealousy sparking in Van's dark eyes.

"My favorite *Van*-pire," he said in a teasing voice, as he opened his door and climbed into the Porsche beside Mary Ellen. "Hey, Mathias, you'd better watch out for this one," he called. "She bites."

Vanessa smiled softly and took Harry Mathias's arm. "My turn's coming, my dear Preston," she said under her breath, as Pres and Mary Ellen drove away. "Just you wait and see."

"Well, what do you think?" Mary Ellen asked Angie, as they stood in front of the second-floor hallway window and looked out. On the brown, frostbitten lawn under the window a half-dozen girls and two or three boys dressed in fleecy warm-up suits were practicing cheers on the Tarenton High lawn.

Angie considered. "I think Ardith is right," she said, thoughtfully, her eyes on the group. "A couple of those kids are good enough to join the squad right now, if you ask me." She laughed a little. "I mean, I hate to say it, but it's the truth."

Mary Ellen shook her head determinedly. "One or two of them are pretty okay, but I wouldn't go so far as to say they could make the squad."

"Well, I would," Angie insisted, taking Mary Ellen's arm. "Look at that guy over there, that dark-haired one at the bottom of the pyramid. What a *bod* he's got. And he's got top moves, too — crisp and precise. Real sure of himself."

Mary Ellen studied the boy that Angie was pointing to. He was muscular and good-looking and he definitely had style. "Well, their pyramid's offsides, but *he* isn't so bad," she agreed finally. She smiled. "In fact, I wouldn't exactly mind helping *him* work out for a day or two. Why, his moves are almost as good as Pres's."

Mary Ellen smiled again, to herself, thinking about last night. She and Pres had driven around Narrow Brook Lake and up to the hill, talking animatedly about going to see Paul Howell in a day or two. And then Pres had parked in the dark shadows of the pine trees, and held her and kissed her competently and with a great deal of dedication to the task. The shook her head with bemusement, remembering her response, the breathlessness, the warmth that flooded her. It had been good, there was no doubt about it — even if it wasn't quite as good as it always was with Patrick Henley. In fact, if she was going to be honest she ought to admit right here and now that probably nothing would ever be quite as good as it was with Patrick. But what she had felt last night with Pres was close enough, she had decided, especially when she considered all the *other* good things about him. And that was what she had to keep in mind — all those other good things. They all added up, every one of them. And Mary Ellen was extremely good at keeping track of things that added up.

Angie was pointing out the window again. "And look at that dark-haired girl," she was saying, with reluctant enthusiasm. "The really pretty one. Wow — what energy she's got! And she really knows her stuff, too, Mary Ellen. Watch what she's doing now!"

Just at that moment, the dark-haired girl, lithe and graceful, executed a perfect — and perfectly effortless — straddle jump. "Amazing!" Angie exclaimed softly, envy in her voice. "I'd have to give her a ten on that one. I don't think any one of us could do any better."

"Eight," Mary Ellen said, turning away from the window and starting down the hall. "Her break was a little uneven. Both you and Olivia could have done that a lot better."

"Oh, come on, Mary Ellen," Angie said, hurrying to catch up with her. "There's no sense in being jealous of these prospects. We'll be gone by the time they're ready to take our places."

"Who's jealous?" Mary Ellen asked casually, stung. "I just think that all of us have more to do with our time right now than spend it fooling around with a bunch of younger kids. After all, nobody set up a clinic for us, did they?" She looked at Angie. "From what you said yesterday, I thought you agreed with me."

Angie nodded. "I did — yesterday. But watching this group, I guess I've changed my mind. I know it's going to take a lot of time to do the clinic, and I'm not sure myself that I want to give up a whole weekend. But I think it's something we ought to do. They're good. And Ardith's right. She's got to get a squad together for next year. It would be a help to her if she could get *some* idea about the kind of material she's going to have to work with." She grinned wickedly. "And anyway, you haven't convinced me that you're not jealous."

Mary Ellen stopped in the middle of the hall and turned to face Angie, her face flushed. "Well, just to prove to you that I'm not," she said, "I'm going to go along with this crazy idea — even though I still think that we have better things to do with our time than baby-sit." She shook her head, thinking of all the things she had to do: schoolwork, modeling at Marnie's, getting her portfolio together, talking to Mr. Howell. And now this. There just wasn't enough time to do it all!

Angie nodded. "Well, I'll have to admit that we've all got a time problem," she said sadly. "Or maybe it's an energy problem, or something. I totally crashed and burned on a calculus test today because I just couldn't make myself study without Chris sitting there, keeping me at it." She made a wry face. "One or two more of those kinds of tests, and I won't have to worry about where I'm going to college. I won't be *going* to college."

On the other side of the lawn, Walt and Pres stood together, hands in the pockets of their jackets, watching the group working out on the grass.

"Mmm," Pres said appreciatively. "Some *body*."

"Somebody?"

"Yeah. That cute little brown-haired girl over

there." Pres pointed. "Some body, wouldn't you say? I mean, even under that warm-up suit, I can tell she's got what it takes. Where's she been all year? How come she hasn't crossed my path yet?"

Walt looked in the direction Pres had indicated. "I'll say," he agreed, with an unaccustomed interest. "You've got a point there. I wonder who she is. She is *some* cute."

Pres smiled. "Well, it doesn't matter to me who she is, body or no body. I've got other things on my mind these days."

"Oh, really?" Walt asked idly. "Who've you got it going with this time?" He looked across the lawn. "Hey, look at that guy," he said, in a speculative tone. "He's not bad."

Pres grinned. "Melon."

"Who?"

"Melon."

"That's what I thought you said." Walt looked at him sideways. "Hey, man, Mary Ellen is Patrick's girl." He stopped, half embarrassed, and looked away. "I mean, maybe they're not going steady or anything, but — "

"Who says she's Patrick's girl?" Pres interrupted reasonably. "Patrick doesn't say so. I mean, I suppose he'd like it if she would agree to date him exclusively. But *she* doesn't say so. In fact, she says she's definitely not Patrick's girl." And she acts like she's available, too, he added to himself, remembering how warmly Mary Ellen had responded last night when he had kissed her. Spirit and energy. He could feel the electricity just thinking about it. Yes, that was exactly how to describe her, especially in the love category. Spirit and energy — electricity. That was Mary Ellen Kirkwood to a T.

Walt looked back to the lawn, losing interest in Pres's affairs of the heart. "Well, you ought to know," he said. "After all, you're Patrick's partner. I don't figure you'd do anything to break *that* up. Say, would you *look* at that guy," he added admiringly. "He's super!"

"What guy?"

"The one with the dark wavy hair and the tan. Mr. Muscles, U.S.A."

Pres looked, just as a tall, dark boy did three perfect flips and a roll. "Mmm," he said admiringly. "Looks like we've got some interesting competition there, wouldn't you say?"

"No competition as far as I'm concerned," Walt shrugged. "By the time he's ready to take my place, I'll be long gone." Maybe, he thought, hunching his shoulders against the cold. Maybe I'll be gone — to State or to New York. The meetings with the agent had been promising, and Walt's parents were seriously considering a preliminary offer. But on the other hand, there was Olivia. His gaze swiveled back to the dark-haired girl.

"Right," Pres said. "Long gone." He laughed and squeezed Walt's arm. "Well, if it's all the same to you, even if I'm not in the market just now, I still prefer that girl to that guy."

"Absolutely," Walt said, watching her as she stepped lightly and easily onto the shoulders of the dark-haired boy. "That goes for me, too."

Just at that moment, Olivia and Nancy came up. "Hey, is this the matinee?" Olivia asked. "Who's selling tickets? Where's the popcorn?"

"This is it," Walt said, slipping his arm comfortably around Olivia's shoulders. "What do you think?"

"I'll take two of that guy with the dark hair, that's what *I* think," Nancy said with a little laugh. "Where in the world has he been all my life?"

Pres nodded. "Exactly what I was saying to Walt about that cute girl with the brown hair over there." The girl jumped down from the boy's shoulders and did a handstand, toes pointed, back steady and perfectly arched. "Boy, is she good!"

"Yeah," Walt said, watching her with interest. "In fact, I'm beginning to think that Ardith's notion about a clinic isn't so bad after all. And I'm going to volunteer to coach the redhead — one-on-one." Laughing, he ducked Olivia's quick, playful swing.

"Taking notes?" Vanessa asked, coming up to them. "Picking out your favorites for next year's squad?"

"Oh, come off it, Van," Pres said good-naturedly. He grinned at Walt. "Actually, Walt and I were just doing a little lunch-hour girl-watching, and Olivia and Nancy came along to make sure we did a good job."

Van surveyed the group on the lawn. "It's interesting, isn't it?" she murmured, after a minute.

"What's interesting?" Pres asked.

"How times change," Van said. She opened her bag and took out a spiral notebook and began to jot something down. "I mean, this year's team is on its way out — sort of like yesterday's news. What's out here is the *next* Tarenton squad." She put her notebook away with a bright smile. "Now, isn't that a fascinating angle for a story? I wonder what my editor's going to think of it."

CHAPTER

Angie stumbled once more, halfway through the routine, and Ardith Engborg gave a short, sharp blast on her whistle.

"I take it all back," she said with a disgusted look on her face as the cheerleaders gathered around her at the edge of the floor. "Maybe you all have patched up the differences you've been having with each other, but you haven't patched up the problems you have with your routines. That last effort showed *no* effort at all!" She looked around the group. "Pres, you're moving about a beat too fast. Slow it down and put a lid on some of that energy you've got today. Angie, you've got to snap it up! Your turns on that drill are way too slow. You're like a turtle out there!"

Angie wiped her face with a damp towel and tossed it onto a bleacher seat, looking unhappy. "Okay, okay," she muttered bleakly. "I hear you.

Let's try it again. I'll get it right this time."

Ardith gave her a quick look. "Angie, why don't you try turning off your mind and just letting your body do all the work?" she asked, in a softer voice. She glanced around at the other cheerleaders. "In fact, that would be my advice to all of you. I have the feeling that whatever's on your minds is interfering with the way you move your bodies."

Pres winked broadly at Mary Ellen, who was standing next to him. "Doesn't look to me like anything's interfering with the way you move *your* body," he said to her, under his breath.

Mary Ellen blushed and looked flustered. Ardith glanced up sharply, with an ironic half smile. "Well, I'm glad to hear that you've noticed the way Mary Ellen's moving, Pres," she said. "Maybe this time you'll keep your eyes on her and count out the beat to be sure you get it right." She waved her hand and blew her whistle, with another glance at Angie. "Okay, everybody back out on the floor. One more time!"

Back out in the middle of the floor, Angie lined up next to Olivia and tried to concentrate on the new "Victory" cheer they'd been working on for the last several practice sessions. But it was hard. Chris's familiar face — the face she loved — kept coming into her mind, and the sound of his voice last night on the phone still echoed in her ears, no matter how hard she tried to push it out and focus on the cheer.

"I'm trying to explain, if you'll just give me a minute and listen," he had said. That was after he had told her that he and his parents were flying to Yale next weekend to tour the campus, talk to the admissions officer, and take a look at the dormitories. The news had almost knocked her over. She had been so stunned that she could hardly hear what he was saying over the loud, erratic pounding of her heart.

"I don't really *want* to make this trip to Yale, Angie," Chris kept insisting. "But I've got to act like I do, or Dad is going to make the rest of the year miserable for me. I'm just playing a game with both my parents — just pretending that I'm interested, even though I'm really not." There was a silence on the phone. "Can't you trust me, Angie?"

The hot tears rising in her eyes, Angie had put down the phone without answering. The issue wasn't whether or not she trusted Chris. She had seen pictures of the Yale campus. She knew how beautiful it was, and how smart the girls were there. And she knew beyond the shadow of a doubt that once Chris saw how strong the programs were, he would decide not to settle for State, where she had already been admitted. Anyway, she couldn't go to Yale, even if she wanted to. Her mother could barely afford to help her as it was. She was going to have to depend on getting some kind of scholarship. And besides, she didn't have the grades for Yale. In Angie's mind, there was no doubt about it. Chris was going to Yale, and when he did, she would lose him. The fear rose inside her like a fog, blocking out everything else.

"Angie," Mary Ellen whispered urgently, to one side of her. "Pay attention. You're out of step." She counted out loud. "One — clap — two — clap — three — clap."

"Sorry," Angie said, trying to catch the rhythm. She shook her head, concentrating on the complicated two — three — two pattern. It wasn't that it was hard at all — just a little bit complicated, and she kept on dropping two whole beats out of the middle. Unfortunately, the part that she was missing was the most crucial to the cheer. That was where she had to hand off to Olivia, before Olivia moved into a quick series of back flips.

Her eyes on Mary Ellen's feet, Angie clapped twice on the next beat, turned quickly to the left, and held out her hand to Olivia. But Olivia wasn't there. Angie knew immediately that she had missed the count again. She stopped in the middle of the routine, looking confusedly around her. There was a thump and the sound of Ardith's whistle, and then silence.

"Ohhh!"

Angie whirled. Olivia was crumpled in a heap on the floor, clutching her ankle, her face gray and twisted with pain.

Walt was there in an instant. "What is it, Olivia?" he asked anxiously, bending over her. "Are you okay? Where does it hurt? Tell me."

"It's my ankle," Olivia said, struggling to sit up. "Oh, Walt," she began to cry. "I think my ankle's broken!"

"Shhh," Walt said tenderly, as Ardith came rushing up. Gently, he pressed Olivia back down onto the floor. "Don't try to sit up just yet."

Shocked, the others were gathered closely around Olivia and Walt. Mary Ellen and Nancy were clinging mutely to one another, and Pres had dropped to his knees beside Walt. Angie could feel the hot pulse of tears in her throat. She stared for a moment at Olivia's twisted ankle and suddenly she knew she was going to be sick.

"Excuse me," she mumbled, bumping blindly into Mary Ellen. Holding her hand over her mouth, her stomach heaving, she ran off the floor toward the locker room.

Ardith pushed everyone aside and knelt down beside Olivia. "Okay, let's take a look," she said, and Walt moved back a little. Carefully, Ardith untied Olivia's tennis shoe and pulled off her white sock, her practiced fingers probing the twisted ankle. "Well, we're lucky," she said, sharp relief in her voice. "It doesn't feel like anything's broken." She watched Olivia's face as she manipulated the ankle. The others waited in tense silence. After another moment she stood up and said, "I'm sure it's just a bad sprain. Can you put any weight on it?"

Walt put his arm around Olivia's waist. "Come on," he said quietly. "I'll help." He pulled Olivia slowly to her feet. "See if you can stand on it."

Gingerly, Olivia put her bare foot on the floor and then grimaced, her face pale and contorted with pain. She swayed dizzily, leaning against Walt.

"I can't walk on it, Walt," she whispered. "It hurts too much."

"Hey, no problem," Walt announced. He scooped Olivia up in his arms and she put one arm limply around his neck, resting her face against his shoulder. "Okay, Ardith, what now?" he asked.

"Carry her to the weight room and we'll get an ice pack on that ankle right away," Ardith said. "It's going to swell, but I'm sure she'll be able to walk on it by morning." She looked around at the rest of the cheerleaders, still standing huddled together in a silent little cluster, stunned by what had happened. "Well, I guess that'll have to be enough for today, squad," she said. She glanced at Mary Ellen. "Tell Angie that we'll work on this routine again tomorrow — until we all get it right. But don't forget that we still have something to talk about. I'll see you in my office in about half an hour."

In the locker room, Angie was sitting on the bench, her shoulders still shaking, when Mary Ellen and Nancy came in. Mary Ellen sat down beside her.

"It's okay, Angie," she said. "It's not broken — just a bad sprain. Ardith says she'll probably be walking on it tomorrow."

Angie looked as if she hadn't heard. "I just don't know how it happened," she said, her voice trembling. "I was counting, like everybody else, but I just kept on missing those beats, and then Olivia — " She buried her face in her hands. "It was all my fault," she moaned despairingly. "It was all my fault!"

"Listen, Angie, you can't blame yourself for what happened," Nancy said. She had stepped out of her shorts and wrapped herself in a towel on her way to the shower. "An accident is an accident. It can happen to anyone, any time. We all know that." She laughed a little. "All I want to know is who's going to tell Olivia's mother. She'll go into hysterics."

Mary Ellen shook her head. "I guess I'll have to agree with Angie," she said. "I saw how it happened. Angie, you were two beats off and Olivia missed your hand and slipped." She patted Angie's shoulder comfortingly. "But what's happened is over. You have to be realistic about how it happened and try not to let it happen again. But you can't let yourself linger over it. Olivia wouldn't want that. And it'll spoil everybody's work if you do."

Angie just sat there, her shoulders slumped wearily, her face disconsolate. "Oh, Mary Ellen," she whispered. "Everything in my whole life is falling apart. First Chris and now this. Everything."

Frowning, Mary Ellen stood up and handed her a towel. From her point of view as squad captain, she felt that Angie had to take a certain amount of responsibility for what had happened. But she also knew that she couldn't let Angie dwell on it too long. And it sounded to her now as if Angie was feeling sorry for herself, something that Mary Ellen couldn't stand.

"Listen," she said grimly, "I know how you feel, Angie. We *all* know how you feel. But sitting around moping over Chris and crying about Olivia isn't going to help matters one bit." She smiled crookedly. "It's certainly not going to mend Olivia's ankle — and probably not your relationship with Chris, either." She tugged Angie to her feet. "Come on, let's take a shower so that we can go talk to Ardith about this silly clinic idea of hers.

"So you've decided," Ardith said cheerfully, from behind her desk.

"Right," Mary Ellen sighed, looking around the group. Olivia was sitting on a chair with her ankle propped on another chair, a couple of ice packs taped around it. Walt was sitting next to her, holding her hand. "I mean, we haven't taken a vote or anything," Mary Ellen went on, "but it seems that a majority of us want to host the clinic." She paused. "But none of us know the first thing about how to do it."

"Right," Nancy added. "We want to do it but we're just not sure what's involved — and especially how much time it's going to take."

"That's what I like," Ardith said dryly, "real, bubbling-over enthusiasm." She looked around. "So how do the rest of you feel?"

"Well, *some* of us are really bubbling over with enthusiasm," Pres said, with a wink at Walt. "Especially after we had a sneak preview of the local talent out on the lawn this afternoon."

Ardith looked at Walt and Olivia. "How do you feel about it?" she asked.

Walt grinned. "I think it's a good idea," he said. "Like Pres said, some of those kids are pretty good."

Olivia looked depressed. "Well, I don't know what I'll be able to do," she said, looking down at the ice packs on the ankle. "I guess it depends on how long I have to be out with this ankle."

"How about you, Angie?"

"I guess so," Angie said glumly, looking away from Olivia. "I mean, I guess it's a good idea."

Ardith nodded. "Well, I'll tell you," she said. "Ordinarily I wouldn't push you into something that all of you can't wholeheartedly support. But I think you all need a picker-upper — something to take your minds off yourselves and your various troubles. I know that a few of you aren't sold on the idea, but I'm going to take the chance that you will be, once we get started."

Pres leaned forward, elbows on his knees. "What do we do to get started?" he asked.

"Well, I've checked the school calendar," Ardith said, checking some notes on her desk pad. "It looks like the weekend after next is the best time. And that'll give us a number of days for advance publicity, if we can get the school newspaper to cooperate."

"That shouldn't be much of a problem," Olivia said to Walt. "When Vanessa hears about the clinic she's bound to want to make something out of it — something unpleasant, I mean."

Mary Ellen looked at Ardith. "What do we do?" she asked. "I mean, what do people do at a cheerleading clinic?"

"Well, usually, a clinic runs all day Saturday," Ardith answered, with a smile. "We'll handle it like our daily practice sessions, with warm-ups first, and then instruction on cheers, like a class, with everybody out on the floor. Of course there will have to be a lot more emphasis on fundamentals — movement patterns, basic dance formations, exercise programs, things like that — than we usually have in our workouts. In the afternoon, we can divide up into smaller groups and do some one-on-one work. You can take turns handling part of the instruction in the morning, and in the afternoon each of you can be assigned to handle one of the smaller groups." She looked at Olivia. "Olivia, maybe you can help me observe. I want to make notes and get a good idea about these kids' abilities."

"What cheers are we going to teach?" Nancy asked. "I mean, are we just going to teach the standard stuff? Or do we have to give them our special routines — the ones we've worked out ourselves?" Nancy had always had an interest in developing new cheers, and she had helped to design many of the cheers the squad had used all year. For her, designing a cheer was just like choreography, and she wasn't sure that she liked the idea of sharing the work they had done with people they really didn't know — in spite of the fact that some of them were going to be next year's cheerleaders. After all, nobody had given *them* any special routines. They'd had to do all their own choreography.

"I'm going to leave the cheers up to all of you," Ardith said, looking around. "You can decide how you want to do it. But whatever you decide, it would probably be a good idea to write down a list of the cheers you want to teach, and who's going to teach which cheers."

"Right," Pres said, thinking out loud. He looked intrigued by the whole thing. "And then the next thing we ought to do is figure out in what order we're going to teach the cheers. It wouldn't be exactly fair to the kids to give them a really difficult routine to start off with. In fact," he added, with a glance at Olivia's ankle, "it would probably be dangerous."

"Okay," Mary Ellen said, feeling that she ought to take charge of things. After all, she *was* the squad captain. "Let's assign a committee to decide which cheers we're going to teach, and in what order."

"I'll volunteer for that," Nancy said quickly, "if Angie will help."

"I guess so," Angie said. "I ought to be able to do that, at least."

"Right," Mary Ellen said, making hasty notes on the back of her school tablet. "Nancy and Angie on the selection of cheers. And then we'll need somebody to deal with publicity — Angie, maybe you'd handle that. And somebody else — "

"And a party," Walt interrupted excitedly. "We need a committee for the party. I volunteer," he added. "We can have it at my house. On Saturday night."

Olivia stared up at him. "A party?" she asked, with comic suspicion. "Does this sudden enthusiasm for a party have anything to do with that dark-haired girl out there showing her stuff this afternoon?" A relieved ripple of laughter ran around the room. Olivia sounded like her old self again, in spite of the ice packs on her ankle.

Ardith smiled. "Hey, I *like* that idea, Walt," she said, "whatever your motivation is. It would be really nice to give everybody a chance to get acquainted."

"A party," Pres said, looking at Mary Ellen. "That's a great idea."

Mary Ellen nodded, concentrating on her note-taking. As far as she was concerned, this whole thing was getting out of hand. It was going to take two weeks of constant effort to make it all happen. "Right," she said resignedly. "A party. Who would like to volunteer to help Walt with the party?"

CHAPTER

7

"Do I look all right?" Mary Ellen whispered to Pres, for the second or third time. She was wearing a pale beige skirt and sweater, and she had put up her hair in an elegant twist, thinking it would make her look a little older. As an afterthought she had added a pair of long, dangly earrings. She clutched the portfolio of Patrick's photographs under her arm.

"You look fine," Pres said again, touching her arm. "What are you worried about? I mean, Mr. Howell is a nice guy. He's not going to hurt you."

"Yes, but will he want to *help* me? That's what I'm worrying about," Mary Ellen said, tapping her foot nervously. They were sitting in Mr. Howell's outer office, waiting for the door to open.

The phone rang on the receptionist's desk. "You can go in now," she said to Pres and Mary Ellen, smiling.

Pres didn't get up. "I'm not going in," he said, unexpectedly. "I want you to go alone."

"But — but — " Mary Ellen stammered. She had expected that Pres would be there to help.

"You don't need me." Pres smiled. "You can do this all by yourself."

Mary Ellen gulped, remembering her disastrous interview with the woman at the modeling agency in New York. If this meeting was anything like that one, she wasn't sure she would have the courage to go on. Anyway, maybe it was better if Pres didn't come. Then if things went badly, nobody else would know but her.

When Mary Ellen opened the door, she saw that the walls of Mr. Howell's office were lined with pictures and posters — advertisements, photographs, blowups of copy, brightly colored graphic art. Mr. Howell stood up behind his desk, held out his hand, and flashed a wide smile that showed evenly spaced teeth in a dark-tanned face. He was younger than Mary Ellen had expected — in his late twenties, probably — and very good-looking.

"I'm Paul Howell," he said, in a deep-throated voice. "And you must be Mary Ellen Kirkwood." He surveyed her critically, his eyes lingering over her face, her hair. "You're even prettier than Pres said you were."

Mary Ellen blushed. "I — I — thank you," she mumbled. "I'm glad to meet you." She stopped, her mind blank, wondering what to say next. She hadn't expected him to be so young and good-looking.

Mr. Howell gestured toward a plump, overstuffed sofa in the corner of the room. "Come and sit for a few minutes, Mary Ellen. I'd like to get to know you a little better."

Stumbling over a corner of the rug, Mary Ellen sat gingerly on the edge of the sofa. Mr. Howell took the chair across from her and watched her for a few minutes, not saying anything. As the silence lengthened, Mary Ellen grew more and more apprehensive. She wasn't sure whether she should return his stare or look away and pretend he wasn't looking at her or. . . .

"Don't be nervous," he said finally, breaking the silence. "Just sit back and tell me about yourself."

Mary Ellen took a deep breath and tried to relax against the cushions. "What — what do you want to know, Mr. Howell?" she asked.

"Anything you're comfortable telling me," he answered, still studying her. "If I'm going to give you advice about how to 'market' yourself as a model — that's what Pres said you were interested in — I need to know something about you. What you like to do, what bores you, what your ambitions are." He grinned easily. "You know, personal details like that. The kind of details you'd ordinarily never tell a stranger — especially if you insisted on calling him 'mister.' You know, Mary Ellen, my name is Paul, and I'm stuck on it. I kind of like to hear people use it."

Mary Ellen laughed, her nervousness suddenly evaporating under his friendly gaze. She began to talk about herself. It seemed a little difficult at first, especially when she tried to tell him about her feelings about her parents and their little turquoise house, and Tarenton, and cheerleading. But as the minutes went by and she realized that Paul Howell really was interested in her life, the task got easier and easier.

". . . and so what I want to do, most of all," she said finally, after about fifteen minutes of talking about herself, "is to be a high-fashion model and live in a big city and have nice clothes and a nice car and an apartment with a view and — " She stopped, feeling uncertain. Somehow that seemed so superficial, not quite worthy of all the effort it would take to achieve. Was that *really* what she wanted? Or was there something else? Something more?

"And?" Paul prompted, after a minute, watching her.

"Well, I guess there *is* something more to it than that," Mary Ellen said slowly. "I guess what I want more than anything else is to be recognized for my achievements. I mean, I'm really competitive. That's my basic nature. That's why I like cheering so much — it makes me feel like I'm part of the game, somehow. A crucial part. And winning, being the best at what I do, means that people *recognize* me when they see me. They know who I am and what I've done. I like that." She stopped.

"But the trouble is . . . ?" Paul prompted after a minute.

Mary Ellen sighed. "The trouble is that small-town girls in a major city are a dime a dozen. That's what the woman at the agency in New

York City implied, anyway. If I want to be recognized and be really competitive in such a difficult market, I'm going to have to have an image — and not a small-town image, either." She sat up straighter. "A distinctive image that will make me stand out. Make people recognize me and remember me."

"And so that's why you're talking to the director of a marketing firm," Paul said quietly, looking at her over his folded hands. "You want me to help you define an image for you."

"Yes! That's exactly it," Mary Ellen said intently, leaning forward. "There's nobody else in Tarenton who can help. I can't pay you very much, but I'll be glad to — "

"Save your money for your photographs and your wardrobe," Paul said, waving his hand. "And maybe in the end you'll decide that my advice is worth exactly what it's going to cost you — nothing."

"Oh, no," Mary Ellen said, feeling a surge of grateful relief. She hadn't been sure she could afford whatever he was going to charge. "I'll follow your advice, I promise I will. I have the feeling that you're going to be a *very* big help to me."

"I hope so." Paul smiled. He looked at her for another moment. Then he said abruptly, still smiling, "Take down your hair."

"What?" Mary Ellen asked, startled. "What did you say?"

"You heard me," he said gently. "Take it down, Mary Ellen. And take off those earrings, too."

Puzzled and a little hurt, Mary Ellen began to unpin her hair. "Don't you — don't you like it like this?" she asked. "I thought it made me look older."

"It does," Paul said simply. When she had taken it down he stood up and came over to the sofa. He reached down and put his hand under her chin and tilted it up, studying her face. And then he took a handful of her hair and lifted it, holding it against her cheek. After a moment he dropped it and turned away. "Did you bring your photographs?" he asked.

Hastily, Mary Ellen opened her portfolio. "Yes," she said. "They aren't very good, but. . . ."

"Let me be the judge of that," he said, in a kindly voice. "Now, if you don't mind, I'd rather you just left the photographs. I'll give you a call in a few days, after I've had a chance to look at them and think about the advice I want to give you."

Mary Ellen stood up, feeling dismissed. "Did — did I say something wrong?" she asked tentatively.

Paul looked at her and shook his head. "No, of course not," he said, with a little smile. And then he added, "Pres shouldn't have told me that you're pretty. He should have said that you are beautiful."

"And then what?" Angie asked curiously, sitting cross-legged in front of the Goldsteins' fireplace.

"And then nothing," Mary Ellen said, with a

half-despairing smile. "That was two days ago, and I haven't heard from him since." She laughed a little sadly. "If you want to know the truth, I guess I've given up hope that anything is going to come of it."

"Well, give him time," Nancy said, reappearing with a large bowl of popcorn in one hand and a pitcher of hot cider in the other. She set down the popcorn in the middle of the floor where Mary Ellen and Angie were sitting. "Guaranteed calorie-free," she said to Angie, who was hungrily eyeing the bowl.

Angie sniffed. "I smell butter," she said suspiciously.

"A figment of your imagination," Nancy declared. "At this point in the day, *everything* smells like butter to you." She sat down and poured out mugs of hot cider. "Well, where do we start?"

"I'm sure *I* don't know," Mary Ellen sighed. "I don't know anything about how to handle a cheerleading clinic, and I'm not sure I want to learn, either. I've got enough to think about, worrying how I'm going to get my history paper done with the game tonight." The Tarenton Wolves were playing Garrison tonight, in the Tarenton gym, and warm-ups began at six-thirty.

"I understand how you feel," Angie said, scooping up a handful of popcorn. "But the fact remains that we've got to put together a list of the cheers we want to teach at the clinic next week." She stuffed the popcorn into her mouth and pulled out a notebook. "I've brought our practice book, to give us something to think about."

Mary Ellen reached for the book and began to leaf through it. "You know, I'd forgotten some of these cheers," she said, smiling a little. "Do you remember the 'Vocabulary' cheer?" she asked. "We haven't done that one in a long time — since the day Walt got so excited that he got it entirely backwards and threw us all off."

Nancy laughed and leaned over to look through the book with Mary Ellen. "Look, here's that crazy 'Beat 'Em' cheer that we stole from Deep River. That's another one we haven't done lately. Remember how Olivia swiped that cheer? It was pouring down rain, and she sat right in the middle of the field and started taking notes while the Killer cheerleaders were doing the cheer. And later one of the girls from Deep River came over and tried to take Olivia's notes away from her."

"I remember," Angie said, laughing. "And Pres acted so sweet toward the poor girl that he totally confused her and she forgot what she came for. Let's be sure to put that one on the list. Compliments of the Deep River squad."

The girls laughed, and for the next hour they worked happily, constructing their lists. Finally, Mary Ellen glanced at her watch.

"I can't believe it," she gasped. "It's after five, and I promised Mom I'd fix supper for Gemma tonight, before the game. I've got to go."

Nancy shook her head disbelievingly. "Where has the time gone?" She stared at the lists spread out on the floor. "Just *look* at everything we've done! Why, we've got enough material here for *two* clinics."

Angie laughed softly, looking from Mary Ellen to Nancy. "You know something?" she said. "Just thinking about these cheers and remembering what happened at all those games makes me feel really good. Not so much about being a cheerleader, exactly, as being a part of a team." She was quiet for a minute. "Do you know what I mean?" she asked.

Nancy nodded, pulling her knees up to her chin and wrapping her arms around her legs. "You know, lately I really haven't *thought* much about cheerleading. I mean, it's just something I *do*. I've had so many other things on my mind — like Eric — and the squad has just sort of faded into the background."

"Maybe we've been taking ourselves for granted," Mary Ellen said, considering. "After all, it's getting late in the season, and we know that we're all going to be doing something else next year, and — "

"Maybe that's why we really ought to work on being a team again," Angie interrupted. She looked at the lists of cheers that littered the floor. "And maybe this clinic is just what we need to help us feel that way." She laughed. "Pres would say, 'Like wow, how profound.' "

Mary Ellen looked skeptical. "Well, I don't know about that," she said. "But this afternoon *was* fun. I'm sorry I have to leave." She reached for her jacket. "I'll see you guys tonight."

Nancy followed her to the door. "Listen, Mary Ellen, I'm afraid I'm going to be just a little late for warm-ups tonight," she said, once they were out of Angie's earshot. "Eric is taking me out for supper, and he can't get here until swim practice is over."

Mary Ellen looked troubled. "You know how Ardith feels about any of us being late for warm-ups," she said warningly.

"Yes, I know," Nancy said. "But it really can't be helped. We've just *got* to talk about this college thing."

"Well, okay," Mary Ellen said, hugging her. "I'll cover for you as long as I can. But try not to be too late. Ardith can be a dragon when she's mad."

Olivia had just come out of the library, swinging clumsily along on her crutches, when Vanessa caught up with her. "Staying late?" Vanessa asked sweetly. "Catching up on your homework?"

Olivia sighed and shifted her book bag. Walt was picking her up and she didn't want to keep him waiting. They were going to get something to eat before tonight's game. She really didn't want to take the time to talk to Vanessa Barlow, of all people. "Hello, Van," she said, without stopping. "What's on your mind?"

Vanessa fell into step beside her. "I understand that there's going to be some sort of cheerleading clinic in a couple of weeks," she said. "I just wanted to ask one or two questions, that's all. It's for a feature story that I'll be doing for the paper, about the clinic."

"Like what questions?" Olivia asked. She didn't trust Vanessa. Vanessa treated the truth like a snake — she could twist anything so that it wasn't even recognizable.

"Well, like the purpose of the clinic, for starters," Vanessa said, taking out her notebook.

"Oh, that's easy," Olivia said, relieved that Vanessa was asking something straightforward for a change. "There are a lot of talented kids around, and the squad wanted to give them a chance to learn some cheers, so that when the time comes for tryouts, everybody can do their best."

Vanessa scribbled intently. After a minute she asked, without looking up, "Is there any truth to the rumor that this clinic is really a way for the squad to handpick next year's cheerleaders?"

"What?" Olivia asked. She felt as if Vanessa had just jabbed her in the stomach. "Where'd you get that crazy idea?" she demanded indignantly.

"Oh, I don't know," Vanessa said, with a vague wave of her hand. "Some of the kids are talking, that's all." She grinned. "You know, you hear stuff in the halls all the time. No reporter wants to repeat a rumor that isn't true, so I just thought I'd ask, that's all."

"Well, it's a stupid thing for people to talk about," Olivia said hotly. "That's not what the clinic's for at all."

"So you deny the rumor," Vanessa said, capping her pen.

"Of course I deny it," Olivia exclaimed. "It's a ridiculous rumor."

"That's all I wanted to know," Vanessa said smoothly. She put her notebook away. "Can I help you out to the parking lot? You look awfully tired from hobbling around on those crutches all day." She shook her head. "Poor Angie," she crooned. "She must feel just terrible, causing you all this pain."

"I don't need any help," Olivia muttered. Where had Vanessa managed to find out how the accident had happened? And what was she going to write in her story about the clinic?

"Van said what?" Pres asked, stalling for time.

"She said that she and Harry Mathias had seen you and Mary Ellen out on a date the other night," Patrick repeated intently. He was leaning against his garbage truck parked in Pres's driveway. "Is it true?"

Pres sighed and stole a furtive glance at his watch. It was nearly seven and he was already late for pregame warm-ups. Ardith would be furious with him for being late again. "Van's a troublemaker," he said wearily. "I wish I had a dollar for every nasty rumor that girl's started this year. We could use the money to buy another truck."

"I know all about Vanessa Barlow's rumors," Patrick said. He was wearing the white coveralls he always wore on his route, and a pair of heavy leather gloves. "I just want to know whether it's only Vanessa making more trouble or whether it's true, that's all."

Pres squared his shoulders. "Okay, so it's true," he said belligerently. "So Mary Ellen and I *did* go out for a pizza the other night. So what?"

"And then?" Patrick asked. His voice was low and calm.

"And then none of your business, Patrick Henley," Pres snapped.

"Did you kiss her?"

"I said it's none of your business."

Patrick looked at him for a long moment. "I think it is," he said quietly. "I think it *is* my business."

"Oh, come off it, Henley," Pres said, trying to make his voice sound teasing. "Everybody knows that Mary Ellen's attracted to you, but she's just not . . . not. . . ."

"Just not the type to get seriously involved with a garbage man, huh?"

Pres bit his lip and started to move toward his car. It was really getting late. "You said it," he muttered, "not me."

Patrick pushed himself away from the truck and walked toward Pres, hands in his pockets. "You know, Pres," he said thoughtfully, "I've always respected you. You've got class, and I respect class. You've taken a lot from your old man about cheerleading, and you've done a super job helping to get this moving business off the ground. I really like being your partner, and it would be great if we could go on being partners for a long time to come." He paused and pulled off one glove. "But I just have one thing to say to you about Mary Ellen."

"Oh?" Pres asked suspiciously, half turning toward him. "And what's that?"

"This," Patrick said, and swung a heavy right straight into Pres's left eye.

CHAPTER

Ardith looked impatiently at her watch. "Well, where is she?" she demanded, tapping her foot. Ardith and Mary Ellen were standing at the edge of the gym floor, watching the basketball team in their warm-up suits, going through pre-game drill. The sharp thunk! thunk! of balls hitting the floor and the backboards echoed in the half-empty gym as the spectators began to fill the bleachers. Olivia was sitting in the bleachers behind the cheerleaders' bench, her crutches on the seat next to her. She looked glum. Her mother was sitting beside her. Walt and Angie were already out on the corner of the floor, oblivious to everything else, doing two-person stretches. Nancy and Pres hadn't gotten to the gym yet.

Mary Ellen twisted uncomfortably under Ardith's sharp gaze. "Nancy said she was going out to eat with Eric. But I'm sure she'll be here in just a few minutes," she added hurriedly. "She promised she wouldn't be *very* late."

"*Any* late is very late," the coach grumbled. "It's your responsibility as squad captain, Mary Ellen, to get your team members here on time." Ardith gave Mary Ellen a dark frown. "Well, she'd better show up soon, that's all I've got to say. It's bad enough to have to go on without Olivia tonight. If Nancy doesn't appear, we're *really* in trouble. And *where* is Pres? Wasn't he late last week?"

"I don't know where he is," Mary Ellen mumbled, still thinking about Olivia and Nancy. Without Olivia, they had to revise all their cheers, and Nancy was crucial to every one of them. What would they do if she didn't show?

At that moment Ardith glanced up and saw Pres coming toward them. She shook her head and groaned. "Oh, no! What happened to you?"

Mary Ellen turned around. "Oh, Pres!" she wailed. "Your poor eye!" She ran toward him and put one arm around his neck, touching his face gingerly with her fingers. His left eye was black and puffy and there was a long, open cut along his cheek. "What happened, Pres? You look awful!"

Pres pushed her away. "What happened?" he muttered, holding a small plastic bag of ice to his swelling eye. "Patrick Henley, that's what happened." He sat down heavily on the bench. Walt and Angie came up to stare at him, open-mouthed, and Olivia leaned down over his shoulder. He laughed shortly. "You might say that I got hit by a garbage truck."

"A garbage truck? Patrick?" Her hands flying to her mouth, Mary Ellen sat down limply on the floor in front of the bench. "Patrick Henley did *this* to you?"

Walt snickered. "What did you do to *him*? That's what I want to know. Does he have the match to that one?" he asked about the black eye.

Pres shook his head. "Never got to lay a hand on him," he muttered, half ashamed. "He took me by surprise. We were just standing in the driveway talking and wham! he hit me."

Mary Ellen felt like crying. "I can't believe it," she whispered. "Why did he do it?"

Pres glared at her. "Can't you guess?" he demanded. "Dear little Van blew the whistle."

"You mean, she told him that — "

Pres nodded. "Right," he replied bitterly. "And you might say that he was just a little ticked off." He stared at Mary Ellen. "Patrick seems to think that you're in his territory."

Ardith bent over and pulled the ice pack away from Pres's eye. "Can you see out of it?" she demanded, touching his cheek.

"Just barely," Pres said, flinching from the pressure of her fingertips.

Walt looked at Pres. "Not by the end of the game, you won't," he said matter-of-factly. There was an I-told-you-so grin at the corners of his mouth. "It'll be swelled shut in another half hour."

"Doesn't matter," Ardith said crisply, handing the ice pack back to Pres. "You're going to cheer anyway. It wouldn't matter if you were blind in *both* eyes." She turned to Mary Ellen, who was still sitting, dumbfounded, on the floor. "We start warm-ups in two minutes," she said, "Nancy or no Nancy."

Mary Ellen just sat, staring at Pres, the tears threatening to spill over onto her hot cheeks.

"Come on, Mary Ellen," the coach growled. "Snap out of it!" She shook her head, muttering to herself as she walked back to her place on the bench. "One on crutches, one out to supper, one half blind. It's going to be a long night."

Breathing in long gasps, Nancy came running up the stairs and down the hall. The tears in her eyes made it difficult for her to see, and she nearly went sprawling as she entered the gym. The game whistle had just blown, the scoreboard clock had started, and the players were all lined up around the center circle, ready for the toss. She had completely missed the warm-up drill.

"Well, it's about time," Mary Ellen hissed through clenched teeth. "You'd better stay away from Ardith's end of the bench, though. She's ready to chop you up into little pieces and feed you to the Grove Lake Grizzlies."

Nancy sank onto the bench next to Mary Ellen. "I'm sorry, Mary Ellen," she whispered. She looked out on the floor. Through her tears, the team was only a blur of white and red suits, and the crowd behind them seemed to fade up and up into the stands, one gigantic sea of faces. A constant, pulsating din of cheering and clapping echoed in her head.

"Hey, are you all right?" Mary Ellen asked anxiously. "Why are you crying?"

"Sure, I'm all right," Nancy mumbled. She felt in her purse for a tissue and blew her nose and wiped her eyes. "I mean, I will be, in a minute or two." She knew that her eye shadow was smeared. But what did it matter? A little eye shadow seemed trivial after what had happened tonight.

Angie leaned forward. "Hey, what's wrong with Nancy?" she asked. Out on the corner of the floor, Walt and Pres were doing a congratulatory cheer for Troy Frederick, who had already scored a basket and a free throw, putting Tarenton's first three points on the scoreboard.

"Eric and I just broke up," Nancy said simply, blowing her nose again.

"Oh, no," Angie said. Her eyes widened. She got up and came to kneel down on the floor at Nancy's side. "Why?"

"Oh, it's this stupid cheerleading clinic, on top of everything else," Nancy said tearfully, against another sudden loud roar from the crowd. "It turns out that Eric's parents are going to be in Hillsborough the same day and he kept on insisting that I come over and spend it with them. But I told him I couldn't because of the clinic. And then he — he — " She broke down, not able to go any further. In the background, the crowd noise swelled louder and louder until it seemed to fill her whole head with its throbbing roar. If only Eric could see things her way, for once. It wasn't *her* fault that she couldn't meet his parents. She hadn't set the clinic date, but once it was set there wasn't a thing she could do about it. Anyway, it was her obligation to do her part for Ardith and for the squad.

Mary Ellen patted her shoulder sympathetically. "That's really rough," she said. "I mean, really. Couldn't you work out some kind of compromise?"

"Eric doesn't compromise very well," Nancy said, trying to get control of herself. Truthfully, it wasn't just the clinic thing — they might have worked that out. The real problem was that Eric was still smarting from her continued refusal to change her college plans and enroll at Hillsborough, so they could be close to one another. And *that* was something *she* couldn't compromise on, no matter how she tried to work it out with herself. No matter whether it meant losing Eric for good. And now it looked as if she had.

The crowd roared again. "Say, what's going on down there?" Ardith yelled at Mary Ellen, standing up at the end of the bench. "Don't we have any cheerleaders? Get your squad out there on the floor, Mary Ellen. Come on, move!"

Mary Ellen reached for Nancy's hand. "Come on, Nancy," she said. "We've got to get out there and cheer."

"I can't," Nancy said miserably, running her hand through her mussed hair and thinking about her smeared eye shadow. "I'm a mess. I've got to get to the locker room and redo my makeup before I can go out there."

"Forget it," Mary Ellen said, yanking her up unceremoniously. "We're short Olivia already. We *need* you." She turned to the others. "Okay, gang! 'Fever'! Everybody up!" And she ran out onto the court, a brilliant smile on her face, as if the only thing that mattered in the whole world was inciting the Tarenton fans to a near riot.

Out on the floor, Nancy fell blindly into her place in line, next to Pres. When he saw her, he turned to grin. "Glad you could make it," he said dryly.

Nancy stared at him, startled. His left eye was a brilliant blue-green, with a black circle around it. "Pres! What happened to you?"

"Got hit by a garbage truck," he said cheerfully, holding out his hand to her.

"You mean Patrick Henley *hit* you?"

"Do you know any other garbage men?" Pres asked. "Come on, let's cheer!"

Nancy shook her head, uncomprehending. In the bleachers, she could see Olivia, her crutches beside her, both hands raised confidently in a victory sign. Olivia, Angie, Pres and Patrick, she and Eric — the whole world was falling to pieces!

In front of Nancy, Mary Ellen stamped her feet and chanted, "Got spirit?" to set the rhythm.

"Let's *hear* it!" And then the whole squad swung into the "Fever" cheer, taking the entire gym with them. The noise was deafening.

> "We've got the fever!
> We've got the beat!
> We've gonna give you
> A victory treat!
> Beat, treat, treat, beat!
> We're gonna give you
> A victory treat!"

Nancy stumbled clumsily on the first sidekick and missed the hand-clap pattern at the end of the second line. But after that, she found her body taking over for her, her blood surging as it always did with the thrill and excitement of being on the floor with the other cheerleaders, in the passionate heat and excitement of the game. It was something she loved with every bone in her body, and for the few minutes of the cheer, the words thundering through the gym almost blotted out the misery of Eric's final words to her: "If the squad means more to you than I do, I hope you'll all be very happy together. You won't be seeing me again."

On the other side of Nancy, Pres went through the routine automatically. His swollen eye throbbed and the scratch on his cheek stung from sweat. But he could still see out of the other eye, and he scanned the stands for Patrick. Usually he sat about three rows behind the cheerleaders

— unless he had to take pictures, in which case he would be somewhere on the floor. But he wasn't anywhere to be seen.

> "We're gonna give you
> A victory treat!
> Banana splits!"

Pres did the splits that he and the others always did at the end of the "Fever" cheer and trotted off the floor, hoping fervently that Patrick had stayed away from the game. Of course, that was only postponing the inevitable, he had to admit, as he rested on the bench and watched Willie Johnson race down the floor and slam-dunk a hot one. He was bound to see Patrick sooner or later. But by that time he would have decided whether to bow out gracefully and not date Mary Ellen, or whether he ought to make an issue of it. This wasn't an easy decision. He had the feeling that if he *did* decide to make an issue of it, it would mean the end of his moving-business partnership with Patrick. He sighed. That would be a real shame. It looked like they had a good future together — assuming, that is, that Pres didn't give up the business completely and go off to Princeton, the way his parents wanted him to. Was there a future with Mary Ellen? Pres sighed again, remembering how warm and appealing Mary Ellen had been the other night when he kissed her. He couldn't remember *when* things had ever been so complicated.

To the crowd's delight, Mary Ellen stayed out

on the floor after the others had left to do one last pike and a flip. She was graceful and energetic, and she could jump higher than any of the other cheerleaders. She smiled and blew kisses at the crowd as she ran back to the bench, loving their roar of appreciation and the idea that everybody was looking at her. Especially tonight, with the horrible thing that had happened between Patrick and Pres. What in the world had gotten into Patrick? she thought angrily, as she sat down beside Nancy. He had no right to attack Pres, no right at all. It was all Vanessa's fault, really. After the game, when Pres took her home, she was going to tell him so. And if Patrick ever tried to see her again, she was going to tell him exactly what she thought about such barbaric behavior. Really, he had acted like a little kid who couldn't restrain himself. But someplace deep down inside her there was the tiniest little glimmer of self-satisfaction, burning in spite of all Mary Ellen's efforts to put it out. It was the first time in her whole life that one boy had hit another boy because of her.

"I'm going to ride home with Walt, Mother, and that's all there is to it," Olivia said, hobbling on her crutches toward the Jeep, where Walt was waiting for her.

"This is absolutely out of the question, young lady," Mrs. Evans snorted, following along behind her. "Why, you'll catch a horrible cold, riding in that open Jeep with no windows. And with your ankle and all. . . ."

"My ankle won't mind a little cold, Mother," Olivia sighed patiently. "After all the ice packs I've worn for the last couple of days, I imagine it will think this is summer." Walt opened the door for her with a smile and helped her hoist herself in. "Good-night," Olivia waved through the window. "I'll see you in the morning."

"I'll be waiting up, don't you forget it," Mrs. Evans called warningly. "And no loitering out in front of the house! You come in the minute you get home!"

Walt turned on the ignition with a chuckle. "Well, if she doesn't want us to loiter in front of *your* house, let's go loiter in front of *my* house," he said reasonably. "That is, after we've loitered over a hamburger for a half hour or so."

"That sounds like a wonderful idea," Olivia said happily, snuggling as close to him as the gearshift box would allow. "You guys were terrific out there tonight, even without me."

"Oh?" Walt grunted. "Well, I didn't think so. Pres could hardly see; Nancy missed warm-ups, and when she got there she was really only *half* there — and you were sitting up in the bleachers, taking it easy." With a little laugh, he slipped his arms around her. "In fact, with the kind of ragtag cheerleading we were doing out there tonight, I'm surprised that Tarenton won."

"Listen, Walt, I've got something to tell you," Olivia said. "Something odd."

"What's that?" Walt asked, looking down at her hands. "Where are your mittens?"

Absently, Olivia pulled her mittens out of her

pocket and put them on. "Jessica came up to me at halftime and wanted to talk about the cheerleading clinic."

"Jessica?"

"The dark-haired girl," Olivia said patiently. "You know, your special interest. Her name turns out to be Jessica Bennett. She's a junior."

"Oh, yeah," Walt said, shifting noisily for a stop light. He sounded a little more interested. "So that's her name. So what did she want?"

"She wanted to know what she had to do to get chosen for the squad next year," Olivia said, in a puzzled tone of voice.

"Well, that's an easy question to answer," Walt said. "All she has to do is shine at tryouts, that's all. Nothing to it."

"I know," Olivia replied. "That's what I told her. But she acted like there was something else, something having to do with the clinic. Like there was some magic secret that I was supposed to know."

Walt shrugged. "Well, I suppose a little mystery won't hurt. Maybe if the kids think that coming to the clinic will give them a better chance at making next year's squad, we'll have a really good turnout."

"Well, maybe," Olivia said doubtfully. "But I have the funny feeling that there's something else going on. I just wish I knew what it was."

Pres pulled up in the driveway of Mary Ellen's turquoise-blue tract house. He turned off the key in the Porsche's ignition and leaned toward Mary

Ellen. Her face was a pale blur in the dark shadows of the car, and he kissed her lips lightly.

"Mmm," she said in a soft voice, relaxing against the seat and reaching up to touch his eye. "Hurt?"

"Actually, I've got a miserable headache," Pres lied. "I think it would be a good idea if I just went on home and took some aspirin."

To her surprise, Mary Ellen felt a sharp pang of disappointment. She really *had* wanted Pres to kiss and hold her, for a little while, anyway. "Well, we've got plenty of aspirin," she said cajolingly. "And maybe a soda would help, too."

"No, I don't think so," he said, with determination. He pulled her hand away from his face and kissed her fingertips lightly. "Tonight was pretty . . . exciting. I think I'll just go home and get some sleep."

"Sure," Mary Ellen said, as gracefully as she could. "Of course. I understand." She leaned forward and kissed him, lingeringly, and then got out of the car. "I'll see you later. Okay?"

"Sure," Pres said, rubbing his forehead. Maybe he *was* starting to get a headache after all. He started the Porsche. "Sure thing."

At home, finally, in her bed, Nancy pulled the covers over her head and began to cry, deep, painful sobs that wrenched her shoulders and clutched at her lungs. She cried for a long time. She had loved Ben Adamson, and he had been taken from her in a horrible accident. And then she had loved Eric, and now he was gone, too. Would there

102

ever be *anybody* permanent for her? Anybody who loved her enough to make a commitment to her and stick to it? Or was she destined to go through her life loving and losing, losing and loving again, in an endless, agonizing cycle? It didn't seem fair. It just didn't seem fair.

CHAPTER

Getting ready for the clinic had involved even more work than Mary Ellen had imagined. But once over their initial reservations about the event, the cheerleaders were fired by Ardith Engborg's enthusiasm. They began to enjoy the preparations and to look forward eagerly to seeing whether any of the candidates were real prospects for next year's squad.

In fact, Mary Ellen began to suspect as the week went on, getting ready for the clinic was just the thing they had needed to get their minds off the Senior Blues — and off their various personal problems. Olivia was still hobbling around on crutches and the doctor had told her it would probably be even longer than he had thought — maybe two or three weeks — before she could cheer again. Walt was obviously troubled about something, but nobody, not even Olivia, knew exactly what it was. Nancy and Eric still hadn't patched things up. Angie was clearly moping about Chris's upcoming visit to Yale, with a dark and gloomy look that wasn't at all like her usual cheerful self. Worst of all, Pres and Patrick weren't speaking to one another — and Pres hadn't called Mary Ellen since the night Patrick had punched him.

But somehow, in spite of all these personal troubles, working together on the preparations seemed to pull the squad closer. It was even noticeable in their cheerleading. Tarenton had a midweek game against Cedar Point, and their work on the floor was much crisper and more precise and energetic than it had been for a long time. Even Ardith had agreed that they seemed to be over the hump.

Mary Ellen had assigned everybody a specific task to help get ready for the clinic. Nancy was responsible for compiling a master list of the cheers they would be teaching, working from the lists that the girls had made the afternoon of the Northbrook game. Once the list was finished, she and Mary Ellen made assignments, so that all the cheerleaders would have an opportunity to teach one easy cheer and one more difficult one. Angie worked with the school newspaper to publicize the event, and Olivia helped her with the sign-ups.

Judging from the size of the group on the lawn, Mary Ellen had expected that maybe a dozen students would show up. But there turned out to be so much interest that by Thursday, when the sign-up period was closed, the squad had registered seventeen people. And since Walt and Pres were responsible for the party that was planned for Saturday evening, Ardith gave them the registration money to buy soft drinks and snacks.

"You know, Walt, there's something bothering me about this whole thing," Pres said as they came out of the grocery store, arms full of bags of potato chips and cartons of soft drinks.

"Oh?" Walt asked, opening the door of his Jeep and loading a couple of bags into the back. "What's that?"

"Early this morning, before class, a guy stopped me in the hall," Pres said, handing a six-pack of ginger ale to Walt. "He said he was glad we were holding the clinic tomorrow. He said something about it giving him an 'inside edge.'"

"What'd he mean?"

Pres shook his head. "I guess he meant that getting all the extra practice and some tips on cheering would come in handy when it's time for tryouts. But then he said something else that was really odd. I mean, I really didn't understand it. He said that we shouldn't pay any attention to the kids who were upset. 'They don't know a good thing when they see it,' he said."

"Who's upset?" Walt asked.

Pres shook his head. "How should I know?" he replied. "First I've heard about it."

Walt finished stowing the bags and cartons in the Jeep. "You know, Olivia told me something strange last week," he said thoughtfully. "It seems that Jessica — the redhead, the one who's so good — asked her about the clinic. Jessica seemed to have the idea that coming to the clinic had something to do with getting picked as a cheerleader." He laughed as he climbed in. "I told Olivia that I thought it might be a good idea if some of the kids thought that coming to the clinic and working with us would give them a better chance in the tryouts. It might mean a bigger turnout, and more prospects."

"Well, I don't know about that," Pres said. He pulled a shopping list out of his pocket and stared at it absently. "I wouldn't want anybody to get the idea that *we've* got anything to do with the selection process. I mean, Ardith and the judges are the only ones who choose cheer-leaders. And as far as I'm concerned, that's a job they can keep. No *way* am I going to have anything to do with choosing next year's squad." He ran his finger down the list. "Okay, next stop is Bernie's Barbecue. He promised to make us ten pounds of those fantastic barbecued ribs. All we have to do tomorrow night is stick 'em in the oven and warm 'em up."

Walt swung up into the Jeep. "Okay, Bernie's, here we come," he said, turning the key. "This is going to be one great party."

"Right," Pres said, climbing in beside him. He hunched over, shivering. "Do you suppose Jessica will be there?"

"I suppose," Walt said reflectively. He shifted into first gear. Then he said, "Let me amend that. It should be a *terrific* party."

* * *

Early Saturday morning, Walt came into Ardith's office with an armful of red and white pompons. "Here," he said, dumping them unceremoniously in the middle of the floor. "I rounded up all I could find from the members of the Pompon Squad. I hope it's going to be enough."

"If you've got seventeen, that ought to do it," Mary Ellen said, picking up the clipboard with the sign-up sheet on it. She looked at Walt, who was standing with his head cocked, a puzzled look on his face. "Is something wrong?"

"Oh, I guess not," he said, shaking his head. "Something strange just happened, that's all."

"Something strange?"

"Yes. A girl just stopped me as I was getting out of the Jeep and offered to carry the pompons for me. She made a big deal about telling me her name and that she's going to be in the clinic today. She said she was really hoping to do her very best."

"Well, it was sweet of her to offer to help," Mary Ellen said, glancing down the sign-up sheet. "But I don't see anything strange about it."

"I guess it wasn't exactly *what* she said, but the *way* she said it that was strange."

"Oh," Mary Ellen said, with a nod. "Walt, what in the world *are* you talking about?"

"Oh, I don't know," Walt said. "I mean, I had the feeling that this girl was . . . well, you know. Sort of like she was really going out of her way to be nice to me and she wanted to be sure I remembered her."

Mary Ellen laughed. "I still think it was sweet," she said. She put down the clipboard. "Are the mats out on the floor yet? Will you check with Pres and see if he needs a hand?"

After Walt had gone, Angie and Nancy came in, giggling. "Really, *nobody's* acting normally this morning," Angie said. "It's like everybody's got the crazies."

"It really was funny," Nancy agreed. "Maybe they were just trying to be nice, but they made me feel like somebody's grandmother, if you want to know the truth."

Mary Ellen looked from one to the other. First Walt, now Angie and Nancy. What was going on? "What are you two talking about?" she asked.

Angie stopped giggling. "Oh, these two guys out in the parking lot. They looked like sophomores, maybe. I guess they're in the clinic. Anyway, just as we drove up they came running over to the car and introduced themselves and opened the doors for us and made a big fuss about helping us out, like we were royalty or something."

"Actually, it was more like they were Eagle Scouts and we needed help crossing the street," Nancy said. "It was really funny."

Angie nodded. "Yeah, but that isn't all," she said, looking slightly mystified. "Just after we got rid of the two guys, a girl comes up. She doesn't look at all happy, as if she's really ticked off about something. She said that she thought it was an insult to have to butter somebody up to get to be a cheerleader." She frowned. "I couldn't figure out what she was talking about."

"It sounds like the parking lot *was* full of crazies this morning," Mary Ellen said, looking at her watch. "Walt ran into one who thought the pompons were too heavy for him." She pointed to the heap on the floor. "Okay, let's take these downstairs and see if everybody's here. It's almost time to get started."

By eight-thirty, the seventeen clinic participants, most of them wearing warm-up suits over shorts and T-shirts, were gathered in the bleachers. Watching through a crack in the door, Mary Ellen saw to her surprise that while most of the participants were girls, there were six boys in the group.

"Hey, look," she said to Nancy, who was peering underneath her elbow. "There's a whole bunch of boys out there!"

Nancy laughed. "I guess Walt and Pres have done a good job. Everybody knows now that boys can be cheerleaders, too — and good ones." She took another look. "One of those guys is the one we saw on the lawn the other day, Mary Ellen. The guy who looked as if he has a good chance at making the squad. He's sitting at the end of the second row. Somebody told me that his name is Sean. His dad's a salesman or something for Tarenton Fabricators."

"Oh?" Mary Ellen peered out into the gym. It was the same dark-haired, muscular boy who had impressed her so much the week before. She remembered the name Sean Dubrow on the sign-up list. "Oh, yes, definitely." She gave a long sigh. "I *definitely* want him in my group this afternoon."

Nancy stood up. "Hey, I'm the one without a boyfriend," she pointed out with a small smile. "You've got two."

"I don't know how you figure that," Mary Ellen said quietly, thinking about Pres. It had been several days since he had called her. "At last count I think I was down to zero."

Walt joined them, with Pres behind him. "Hey, isn't it time to get out there?" Walt asked. He peered through the door. "Nice-lookin' bunch," he said approvingly. "Hey, Pres, there's Jessica! Things are looking up!"

Olivia hobbled over and leaned against Walt to look through the door. "She's very pretty," she said, in a quiet voice.

"Yes. But the important thing is that she's super-talented," Walt said, his eye glued to the crack. "I really like the way she — "

"What's all this?" Ardith inquired cheerfully, coming down the hall. "I thought we were having a cheerleading clinic this morning, not a peep show."

Walt jerked up, looking sheepish. "Just getting a preview," he grinned.

"Well, that's what we're here for," Ardith said. "To get a preview of next year's possibilities. Now let's get to work."

Mary Ellen and the squad — minus Olivia, who sat next to Ardith on the bench — ran out onto the gleaming maple floor, arms held high, flourishing the victory sign and wearing their biggest and brightest smiles. They had decided that they would start with the Tarenton "Alphabet" cheer in order to get everybody used to using their voices. Then they would bring all the participants out onto the floor for a half hour of exercises to get them warmed up and see how much stamina and concentration they had.

"Hey, gang, we're glad you're here!" Mary Ellen chanted at one end of the line, clapping her hands and jumping up and down.

"Now let's do our 'Alphabet' cheer," Angie shouted, at the other end, as they got ready for the pyramid.

"Gimme a T!" the cheerleaders called, and Mary Ellen and Angie leaped up onto Walt's and Pres's broad backs.

"T!" the kids yelled back. Or at least, Mary Ellen noticed, scanning the stands, some of them were yelling. The others, maybe half of the group, seemed pretty quiet.

"Gimme an A!" the squad called.

"A!"

"Gimme an R!"

"R!"

When the long cheer was over, the squad ran off the floor. "Did you see that?" Mary Ellen asked Angie. "Half of these kids are yelling like crazy. The other half are hardly opening their mouths. I don't understand it."

Angie looked concerned. "I noticed," she said.

"Well, it's pretty early in the morning to be cheering. I'm sure they'll warm up."

"They'd better," Mary Ellen said. She turned to Walt. "Okay, Walt, it's your turn. See if you can get them fired up."

Walt seized the megaphone and ran out onto the floor. "Okay, you've been watching *us* work," he said energetically. "Now it's *your* turn. But I've got news for you. Nobody can do a decent job of leading cheers if he or she doesn't have a set of muscles that just won't quit and lungs that keep on going even after the body's fallen apart. So we want everybody to come out onto the floor for warm-ups. Come on, let's get some action going!"

The students left the bleachers and headed for the floor, some of them shouting and laughing, others moving more slowly, almost reluctantly.

"Hey, come on, everybody," Walt shouted encouragingly. "It's action time! Let's get that blood pumping and those muscles moving! Let's see some life!"

It took a few minutes, but finally Walt got everybody lined up. Then he had them call off their names, one at a time. Mary Ellen recognized a half dozen of the participants from the school hallways and the cafeteria. Others she had seen on the lawn. Mary Ellen noticed that Jessica had stationed herself in the front row, in the very middle, where Walt was leading the exercises. And Sean was right beside her. As the group moved through a set of strenuous calisthenics both of them demonstrated excellent coordination and stamina, and a great deal of bouncy self-confidence.

But the rest of the group was mixed. Some of the prospects seemed to be doing their very best — a few even seemed to be showing off. But others were slow and draggy. They didn't exhibit the spirit that Mary Ellen had expected everyone to have.

After a while, Mary Ellen went to sit down next to Ardith, who was watching intently from the bench. "You know, Ardith, something just doesn't feel right," she said. "But I can't figure out what it is. I mean, Walt is giving it everything he's got, but some of them just aren't responding."

Ardith nodded. "There are some pretty hostile-looking people out there," she said. "That surprises me."

"I thought that everybody who signed up for the clinic would be really *excited* about it," Olivia said, from her seat on the other side of Ardith. "But some of them are acting as though they wished they were somewhere else."

Mary Ellen shrugged. "Well, maybe they're just not interested in being cheerleaders," she said.

"Then why are they here?" Olivia asked. "Why would they want to spend a whole Saturday practicing cheers if they're not interested in being cheerleaders? It doesn't make sense."

Mary Ellen studied the group on the floor. "Jessica Bennett looks like she's happy to be here," she said. "She's really good, isn't she?"

Ardith nodded, studying the group. "She's got a lot of snap, I'd say."

Olivia's crutches fell off the bench onto the floor with a bang, and Mary Ellen bent over to pick them up.

"Just leave them there," Olivia said.

Mary Ellen looked at her. Olivia was watching Jessica now, and her face was pale, her mouth tight. Suddenly a thought came into Mary Ellen's mind. Was Olivia jealous of Jessica? Oh, come on now, Mary Ellen told herself. Olivia is one of the least jealous people she'd ever met. But then she remembered Walt's friendly interest in Jessica. Or was there something more to it than friendliness?

Just at that moment, Walt went up to Jessica and put his hand on the back of her neck, showing her how to adjust her shoulders for one of the exercises. Mary Ellen glanced again at Olivia. Her mouth had tightened into a pinched, narrow line and her shoulders were hunched over.

Ardith stood up and motioned to Walt. "That's enough for warm-ups," she said. "It's time for a break. Let's get everybody back here in five minutes for the first demonstration."

"Hi."

Mary Ellen raised her head from the drinking fountain. The tall, dark-haired boy was standing next to her, watching her with a half-crooked grin, his eyes full of admiration.

"Hi," Mary Ellen said.

"My name is Sean," the boy said. "Sean Dubrow." He had a deep, mellow voice.

"I'm Mary Ellen Kirkwood." For some reason, she felt herself blushing.

"Of course," he said, with a little laugh. "So tell me something I don't know." He put his hand on her arm. "Hey, I'm one of your biggest fans. I know your name, I know where you live, where you work — "

"You'd better watch out for this guy, Mary Ellen," another boy said, coming up behind them. "He's a real legend. A classic."

"Is that right?" Mary Ellen said. She wasn't quite sure what to say next. Sean still had his hand on her bare arm, where her sweater sleeve was pushed up, and his fingers were warm. "Meaning what?"

Sean winked at her. He dropped his hand. "Meaning that I really like having a good time," he said. "Meaning that I'm not inclined to be shy."

Mary Ellen laughed. "Yes, but the question is, Can you cheer?"

"And the answer is *yes*," Sean said simply. He winked at her again and walked away, leaving her looking after him, her mouth half open. He had taken the trouble to find out where she lived and where she worked. Now, what was *that* all about?

CHAPTER

After the break, Sean made it clear that he hadn't been fooling when he said that he could cheer. The cheerleaders did a demonstration of the "Steamboat" cheer, which was one of the easiest ones on their list, and then Nancy and Angie got everybody out on the floor to practice it. Some of the students, especially the younger ones, had a little difficulty with the last movement — the only tricky part. But Sean picked it up the first time. His body was lean and perfect, without an ounce of extra fat. And the muscles that bunched in his shoulders and back were ample testimony that he would be able to lift and carry a female cheerleader easily. On top of that, he had great timing and enormous enthusiasm. In contrast to the two sullen, slow-moving people on either side of him, he was clearly a first-rate candidate.

"He ought to be at the top of your list for next year's squad," Vanessa said quietly, in Mary Ellen's ear. "He looks like a very hot prospect, wouldn't you agree?"

Startled, Mary Ellen jumped up from her place on the bench beside Olivia. "Vanessa! What are *you* doing here? How'd you get in?"

"I didn't know that this was a closed session," Vanessa drawled. She pulled her red sweater down more tightly across her hips and touched one plum-colored nail to a long, dangly earring. "But then you probably didn't realize that I'm here for an important reason," she said. "I'm doing a feature story on the clinic for the paper, and I came to see how things are going." She glanced out on the court with a mysterious smile. "How *are* things going?"

Mary Ellen swallowed. What was Vanessa up to? "Just fine," she lied. "Things are going just fine."

"I'm not sure that everybody agrees with you," Vanessa said, smiling mysteriously. She gestured toward the court, where Angie was standing in frustration, hands on hips, trying to explain to two cynical-looking girls why they weren't getting the move right. "It's obvious that Angie's having a tough time convincing those two that being on next year's Varsity Squad is worth the effort. In fact, I'd say that they are just down-right hostile, wouldn't you?" She pulled a pad out of her huge leather purse and made several notes. "Rather an interesting turn of affairs, isn't it?" she added, musing. "I suppose you thought that everybody would be just *dying* to be a cheerleader."

Worriedly, Mary Ellen couldn't help following Vanessa's gaze. Vanessa was right. The people that Angie was working so hard with looked as if cheerleading was the *last* thing in the world they wanted to do. "Oh, some of them are just a little slow getting started," Mary Ellen said hurriedly. "They'll get into the swing of things before long."

" 'A little slow getting started,' Mary Ellen Kirkwood admits," Vanessa repeated, writing it down. "Thank you, Mary Ellen." She glanced down at Olivia, who was sitting on the bench staring out at the court. "Olivia, my dear, I hope your ankle is getting better. And I *do* hope that Angie and you have patched things up."

Olivia pointedly ignored her. After a minute, Vanessa went on, with a slight smile, "Everybody's saying that you might be out for the rest of the year — and that you might not even be able to cheer *next* year. I was just shocked when I heard it. I couldn't *believe* it." She flipped the page of her notebook. "I'm sure the readers of my feature story would like to know whether your ankle will keep you from trying out for next year's squad."

Olivia looked up with an unreadable expression on her face. "No, my ankle won't keep me from trying out," she said, and then she looked back toward the floor where Walt was demonstrating the right way to do a cartwheel to Jessica and two other girls. When Walt was finished, Jessica executed three perfect cartwheels.

"Oh, I'm *so* glad to hear you're going to be okay," Vanessa said, ". . . eventually." She reached down to pat Olivia's shoulder. "Isn't it just amazing the way these awful rumors get started around this school?" She gave a little laugh. "You can hardly trust anybody anymore."

"Just amazing," Olivia said darkly, not looking up.

Vanessa laughed again and turned to Mary Ellen, pulling a crumpled paper bag out of her big leather shoulder bag. "Well, if nobody has any objection, I'm just going to sit up in the bleachers and watch for a while and see if the group really *does* get into the swing of things. But I wonder if you'd do me a favor." She smiled silkily and held out the bag. "I see that Angie's busy out there on the floor, and I don't want to interrupt her when she's having such a difficult time with those girls. Would you give this to her, please? It's something that her friend Chris left behind last night. At my house."

Mary Ellen stared at her. "Chris was at *your* house?" she asked, before she could stop herself. And then she could have bitten her tongue off. She knew better than to give Vanessa an opening like that. It was like sticking your bare foot into a giant animal trap that had very ferocious teeth.

Obviously, Mary Ellen's question was just what Vanessa wanted. "That's right," she said.

"Chris and I spent the evening playing a little game of — "

Just at that moment, Angie ran up and tugged at Mary Ellen's arm with a worried look. It was obvious that she didn't see Vanessa. "Listen, Mary Ellen," she said, "things are pretty slow. Some of these kids just don't seem to be with it. In fact, a few of them act like they're angry. We've just got to get them steamed up one way or another. How about getting Sean and Jessica to do — "

"Well, Angela," Vanessa said, with a casual smile that showed her white, even teeth. "You're exactly the person I wanted to see." She held out the bag. "I'm sorry for interrupting, but I wonder if you would mind terribly giving this to Chris for me when you see him next. I don't think he meant to leave it."

Angie stared at Vanessa, suddenly wide-eyed. "To Chris?" She took the bag. "What is it?"

"It's his shirt."

"His *what*?" Angie's voice rose up on a high, thin note. Mary Ellen put her hand on Angie's arm.

"His shirt," Vanessa said softly. "He left it at my house last night."

"But what was he — ?" Angie began. Mary Ellen gave her arm a hard, warning squeeze to tell Angie to just take the shirt without asking any questions that would give Vanessa an opening for her painful jabs. But it was too late.

"What was he doing at my house?" Vanessa

121

asked, finishing Angie's question for her. "Was that what you wanted to know? Oh, he just came over for a little visit, that's all. We wound up playing a few rounds of Ping-Pong."

"Ping-Pong?" Angie whispered.

"Yes, that's right," Vanessa replied smoothly. "We'd been playing for a half hour or so, and then we sat down in front of the fire for a little while. It was after midnight, you see, and I think he was feeling a little warm when he took his shirt off. And then he seemed to have his mind on . . . other things. I'm sure he didn't mean to leave it." She gave a tinkling little laugh. "No, I'm *quite* sure he didn't mean to leave it." Carelessly, she brushed a strand of dark hair off her forehead. "Chris really is a *very* good Ping-Pong player, don't you think, Angie? He has such terrific athletic ability. Why, I do believe he's the very best I've ever . . . played Ping-Pong with."

"I guess I wouldn't know about that," Angie said, so low that Mary Ellen could barely hear her. She was clutching the bag, her knuckles white. "We've never played Ping-Pong together."

"Oh, that's too bad!" Vanessa exclaimed. "You've missed something special, then. You know, Angela, you really should have a game with him soon. Before he goes off to Yale, that is."

The kids on the floor had just finished one cheer and were ready to start another. Nancy left the group and ran over to where Mary Ellen was standing. "Are we ready to go again?" she asked.

"Come on, Angie, let's do the 'Catfish' cheer. They've *got* to get charged up with that one."

"Why don't you and Walt and Pres handle it, Nancy," Mary Ellen suggested quickly, glancing at Angie's stricken face. Angie wasn't in any shape to get out there and cheer. "Angie will be back out in a minute."

"Well, okay," Nancy said uncertainly. "But I really wish I could figure out what's wrong, Mary Ellen. Some of these kids are breaking their necks to do a good job. They act like they *want* us to notice them. But some of the others just don't seem to care very much. It's bizarre."

Vanessa laughed a little as Nancy loped back onto the floor. Then she looked more closely at the group. "Oh my goodness, there's Jessica Bennett!" She waved energetically. "Hello, Jessica!"

From the front line, Jessica smiled and waved back.

Vanessa turned to Mary Ellen. "Jessica Bennett's mother is one of my mother's oldest friends, you know," she said smoothly.

"No," Mary Ellen said. "I didn't know." On her scorecard, that was a black mark against Jessica. It might not make any sense to some people, but it made perfect sense to Mary Ellen. There wasn't anybody in the world she hated more — and with more reason — than Vanessa Barlow. And if she were inclined to waver in that hatred, one look at Angie's pale face and Olivia's hunched-over shoulders was enough to confirm it again.

"Yes, Jessica and her brothers are old friends of the family," Vanessa was saying, in a bubbly voice. "In fact, I was talking to her just last week. I told her that I was sure she would make a *wonderful* cheerleader. Exactly right for Tarenton, wouldn't you say? So much energy, vitality, vivaciousness. And look at that jump!"

At that moment, Jessica executed a high straddle jump with flawless ease and grace. It almost looked as if she were flying. Mary Ellen took a deep breath. If the tryouts were tomorrow, Jessica would undoubtedly be selected.

"Why, Olivia," Vanessa went on, looking down, "Jessica is every bit as good as you are right now! Just think how terrific she'll be this time next year, with a little more experience behind her." She hitched her purse up on her shoulder and turned to go. "She's exactly the kind of cheerleader Tarenton needs to take your place as the squad captain, wouldn't you agree, Mary Ellen? And she's absolutely beautiful, on top of all that talent. I'm sure that all the boys will love her." She glanced back out toward the court, where Walt was helping Jessica with a complicated turn. "She certainly does seem to have made a hit with Walt," she added innocently.

Mary Ellen was struggling to control the anger that was churning inside her. "Are you sure you don't have any more time to talk, Vanessa?" she asked tightly. "We certainly don't want to keep you hanging around any longer than absolutely necessary."

"No, I think I've done everything I came to

124

do," Vanessa said, with a satisfied smile. "Angie, I'd really appreciate it if you'd see that Chris gets his shirt back right away. And really, I'm awfully glad to see that so many talented people showed up today, even if they don't all seem to be enjoying themselves. Olivia, you'll certainly have a great deal of competition in tryouts, won't you? Why, who knows? There are so many good cheerleaders out there that Tarenton might even have a *totally* new squad!" She looked around with a careless wave of her hand. "Well, good-bye, all. Have a simply *wonderful* day!"

Nobody said good-bye.

Angie stood staring at the bag in her hand. "Chris's shirt? Chris left his shirt at Vanessa Barlow's house?" She looked as if she was going to be sick.

Mary Ellen swallowed past the lump of anger and raw pain in her own throat. It hurt to see Angie so shaken. "You know Vanessa too well to be taken in by something as flimsy and stupid as this little trick, Angie. There's just got to be an explanation. I mean, Chris isn't *that* kind of a jerk."

"What kind of a jerk?" Angie asked numbly.

"The kind of a jerk who would leave his shirt at Vanessa Barlow's house, that's what kind," Mary Ellen retorted grimly. "Look in the bag she gave you. It's probably something else altogether, and she just told you that story to get you steamed up."

Reluctantly, Angie opened the bag, and looked inside, then closed it again. "It *is* his shirt," she whispered, her eyes tightly shut. "It's the blue-plaid flannel shirt he was wearing when he took me home last night after practice." She looked up, her mouth twisted with pain. "Oh, Mary Ellen, I *knew* I was going to lose him eventually! But I didn't know I was going to lose him to Vanessa! That makes it even harder to bear!" Tears began to run down her cheeks and she wilted down onto the bench as though her legs wouldn't hold her up any longer.

Mary Ellen knelt down in front of her. "Listen, Angie, you've got to pull yourself together. Vanessa is sitting up there in the bleachers, watching. I'm sure she's getting a huge kick out of seeing you cry."

"It doesn't matter," Angie said miserably. She pulled the shirt out of the bag and pressed a sleeve against her cheek. "It even smells like Vanessa's perfume," she whispered. "Oh, Mary Ellen, I can just imagine the two of them sitting in front of Vanessa's fireplace, in that fancy den of hers."

"Don't imagine anything until you know the truth, Angie," Mary Ellen said, trying to be calm and sensible, for Angie's sake. "All you have is Vanessa's version of what happened last night. And you know that you can't trust her to tell the truth. She *wants* you to think the worst. Why, she's perfectly capable of dousing Chris's shirt with perfume, just to make you feel bad." She gestured urgently toward the door. "Listen, why don't you take a break right now and go up to Ardith's office and call Chris? All you have to do is ask him, straight out. He'll tell you what happened. And chances are that it wasn't at all like Vanessa implied."

"I can't," Angie said. She looked very pale and tired. "I can't call him."

"Why not?"

"Because he and his folks left to fly to Yale real early this morning, that's why!" Angie held the bag tightly to her, a tear dripping off her chin. "He's going to be gone all weekend. I won't be able to talk to him until Monday!"

CHAPTER

They took a break for sandwiches and chips and soft drinks at noon in the school cafeteria, where Mrs. Engborg had two tables set up specially for the participants. Mary Ellen, still puzzled over the morning's slow start and the attitudes of some in the group, carried her sandwich over to a pretty girl with short brown hair and freckles, who was wearing a sullen look on her face. Mary Ellen was thinking that maybe, if she asked somebody straight out, she could find out what was wrong. It was worth a try, anyway.

"Hi, I'm Mary Ellen Kirkwood," Mary Ellen said. "Okay if I sit down?"

The girl looked up from her sandwich and then looked away again. She shrugged. "I guess you can sit anywhere you want," she said shortly.

Mary Ellen sat down, surprised. The girl

looked positively hostile. "What's your name?" she asked.

"De De," the girl answered. "De De Handley."

"What year are you?"

"Junior."

"Have you been at Tarenton for a while?"

"No, I just transferred this year."

Mary Ellen sighed. It was beginning to feel like a game of twenty questions — with somebody who didn't exactly want to play. Maybe it was time to get to the heart of things. "Listen," she said. "I'm a little worried about what's happening today." She looked around. At the other end of the table, two boys sitting across from Pres were clowning madly, obviously trying to get Pres's attention. Next to them was a girl who hardly looked up from her plate. "Some of the kids act like they don't really want to be here. Others act like they want to be sure that everybody *knows* they're here. What's going on?"

De De studied Mary Ellen. "Do you *really* want to know?" she asked.

"Well, sure," Mary Ellen said. "That's why I'm asking."

De De put down her sandwich. "Well, actually, I'm glad you asked. I think *somebody* ought to speak up about it. It's not fair."

Mary Ellen looked blank. "What's not fair?"

De De gave her a look. "You know what I'm talking about," she said. "Everybody knows that the Varsity Squad staged this clinic just so they could give their favorites a chance to show off."

129

"A chance to show off?" Mary Ellen repeated. There was a sick feeling in her stomach. She put down her sandwich abruptly.

"It's true," De De said bitterly. "I mean, here you guys are, handpicking next year's squad." She glanced down at the end of the table where the two boys were still clowning noisily. "Some of these kids figure that they'll really do a number for you, butter you up and everything, and they'll be a shoo-in at the tryouts. But the rest of us really resent the idea that the squad would stoop to playing politics. We think it's pretty rotten that you would have anything to do with choosing next year's cheerleaders. We don't think that's your job."

Mary Ellen pushed her sandwich away. She couldn't possibly eat it. "Where did you hear all this?" she asked. As if I *had* to ask, she thought angrily. It looked like another one of Vanessa's tricks.

"Oh, everybody knows it," De De said vaguely. "Jessica told me about it." She laughed briefly, nodding toward Jessica's place across from Walt and Olivia. "Jessica's one of the ones who figures she's got a sure thing going. Just look at her. She thinks that Walt Manners will get her on the team." She laughed again. "And that's pretty ridiculous. She's good enough to make it *without* buttering up anybody."

Mary Ellen stood up. After all their work and their high hopes for today's clinic, everything had gone wrong. "Well, thanks for telling me, De De," she said. She knew that her feelings showed in her voice. "At least *somebody* had the courage to be honest."

De De looked up, a look of surprise on her face. "You mean you didn't know?"

Mary Ellen shook her head. "We planned this clinic in order to give everybody a chance to show his or her best stuff," she said. "Nobody's got any favorites, least of all the cheerleaders. And there are *no* sure things." She looked at Jessica, who was gesturing confidently to reinforce a point she had just made, remembering that Vanessa claimed Jessica as a friend. "There are no sure things at all," she repeated. "Getting to be a cheerleader depends on only one thing. And that's talent."

The other girl looked dubious. "I'd like to believe you," she said slowly. "We're all here because we want to do well in the tryouts. We'd all like a fair chance at making the squad."

"Well, you've got that chance," Mary Ellen said emphatically, picking up her tray. "But only if you get those rumors out of your mind and show Ardith Engborg everything you have. She's the one who selects cheerleaders — she and the judges. We don't have a thing to do with it."

"Do you *really* mean that?" De De asked, her voice softer.

"I *really* mean that," Mary Ellen said. "I wish that you'd talk to some of the others and tell them the same thing."

De De sat still for a moment, considering.

"Okay, I will," she said finally. "I don't know if it'll make any difference, but I will."

"Well, if that's what's going on, the question is, what do we do about it?" Pres asked. The cheerleaders were gathered with Ardith in the coach's office right after lunch. They had just heard Mary Ellen's report of what De De had said. They all agreed that Vanessa was behind it.

"I think we ought to confront this thing," Walt said urgently. "I mean, if we let Vanessa keep on spreading her poison, she could discredit the Varsity Squad. Nobody would ever trust us again."

"Confront it?" Olivia asked bitterly. "How do you confront that kind of thing?" She glanced at Angie, who was sitting, pale and quiet, in the corner. "She hardly ever tells an out-and-out lie. But she certainly makes a lot of implications that aren't true."

"Well, one of us could get up and talk to everybody," Walt said. "We could tell them what we've heard and say it isn't true."

"Right," Pres agreed. "No name-calling or blaming. We just say it isn't true." He turned to Ardith. "Maybe you ought to be the one to do it, Ardith. Maybe they'd be more likely to believe you."

Ardith shook her head firmly. "No. Their problem is with you, not with me. I think one of you ought to address it. And I agree with Walt. I think the best thing to do is to face them with what you've heard and let them know it isn't true." She frowned. "But there *is* something I can do. I can talk to Mr. Howard, the faculty newspaper advisor, and ask him to check Vanessa's feature story very carefully, so that none of these rumors make their way into print."

Mary Ellen nodded, feeling relieved. "Well, then, the question is, Who does the talking?"

"There's no question, Mary Ellen," Pres said quietly. "You're the squad captain. You should be the one to do it."

"Right," Nancy said. "In fact, it would look funny if any of the rest of us did it. But we'll be there," she added. "I mean, we'll be standing right there with you, giving you moral support."

"Thanks," Mary Ellen said dryly. "Will you be there to pick up the pieces afterwards?"

"There won't be any pieces," Ardith said calmly. "My guess is that this will clear the air. I think you'll be surprised at the response."

". . . and in spite of what you've heard, all we want is for everybody to have an equal chance at making next year's squad," Mary Ellen was saying earnestly. She was standing on the court in front of the bleachers, and everybody's attention was riveted on her. She had been talking for ten minutes, trying to make the group understand that the rumors were untrue. "We're not here today to pick out next year's squad," Mary Ellen went on, "although I will confess that Ardith Engborg, our coach, is taking a great interest in the kind of talent she sees here today. But that's because she's got to put together a new cheerleading team for next year, and she's anxious to get a preview of the talent that's going to appear at the tryouts. But that's all it is," she added. "A preview. And we hope that this afternoon, every single one of you will give her the best possible preview, without holding back."

She looked around. The faces that had been sullen and withdrawn looked lively and much more alert, and some of the participants wore relieved grins. For the first time all day, Mary Ellen began to feel that maybe things were going to work out. "Well, are we ready to get to work?" she asked.

"Ready!" the group roared back, and Mary Ellen relaxed.

"Okay, then," she yelled. "Everybody out on the floor for warm-ups! Now!"

As they all raced out onto the court and began to line up, Jessica Bennett walked over to Mary Ellen. Mary Ellen looked at her uncertainly. She had a feeling that Jessica had been used by Vanessa, for Vanessa's own dark purposes. But who knew? Maybe Jessica had her own motives for helping to spread the rumor. Maybe Jessica was like Vanessa — driven by some deep jealousies and inner insecurities to harm those around her.

"I guess I owe you an apology," Jessica said slowly. "To be honest, I probably had a big share in what happened this morning. But I want you to know that I didn't do it deliberately. I heard it from . . . from somebody I trust, and I just thought that others ought to know what I had heard. I'm really glad that everything is straightened out now, and we can have a good clinic."

Mary Ellen studied her intently. Was Jessica telling the truth? Or was she just trying to duck over to the winning side? It was impossible to know. Her eyes were so clear and honest-looking that it was hard to believe that she would lie. Perhaps she really *was* glad that things were straightened out. On the other hand, she was a friend of Vanessa's, and that meant something, didn't it?

"Thanks," Mary Ellen said shortly. No matter how honest Jessica appeared, it would probably be best not to count too much on being able to trust her. "I'll tell the others what you've said."

Jessica looked at her defiantly, and Mary Ellen colored. It was almost as if Jessica could read her mind. "Don't bother," she said. "I'll tell them myself," and she went across the court to where Walt was standing.

After fifteen minutes of strenuous warm-ups, the whole group practiced several more cheers and then broke up into three smaller groups of five or six members each. For the rest of the afternoon, Walt and Angie, Nancy and Pres led the groups through much more difficult patterns that involved more complicated gymnastic routines, while Mary Ellen and Olivia sat with Ardith, watching carefully and making detailed notes on the performances of each of the participants. The change in their attitude had been dramatic. The foot-dragging and hostility of some and the attention-getting antics of others had been replaced by plain, hard work.

By now, Mary Ellen decided, it was almost easy to pick out the eight or nine standouts, the ones who would have a very good chance at making next year's squad. She couldn't be sure, of course, because anything could happen between now and the tryouts. Some who didn't look quite so good today might really benefit from the clinic and surprise everybody. And somebody might transfer in from another school, maybe even somebody with cheerleading or gymnastic experience. Or there might be injuries. You never could tell for sure.

But one thing was perfectly clear. Among the six boys who were here today, Sean Dubrow was without a doubt the very best. Out on the court just a few minutes before, Pres had had him doing spread-eagle jumps — leaping high into the air in a split, arms up. And after that, Sean did the stag jump that Walt had mastered, with his right knee tucked up in midair, left leg straight back. He landed with triumphant perfection, arms flung high and out, back arched like an Olympic gymnast.

"Wow," Mary Ellen said wonderingly. "He's something!"

"Wow is right," Ardith agreed, a look of lively interest on her face. "Looks like we've got a whole handful of prospects." She checked the names she had jotted down. "Handley, Matthews, Stanford, Bennett, Dubrow, Wilson, Cramer, Howard. And maybe a couple of others. Tryouts are going to be interesting, after all." She got up and handed Mary Ellen her whistle. "Okay, Mary Ellen. After another half hour or so, why don't you turn everybody loose for the day. They've worked hard and they must be tired. They deserve that party tonight."

After the coach had gone, Mary Ellen and Olivia sat on the bench in silence for a few minutes, watching. Walt's team of five was practicing right in front of them, and Jessica was in the group. Just now, Walt had them stacked in a high pyramid, with Jessica poised on top, in the place that Olivia usually held. Jessica was wearing a red bandanna headband tied around her lustrous hair, and with her sparkling green eyes and smooth complexion, she was not only graceful, but beautiful as well.

For a minute, Mary Ellen's feeling of admiration was so overwhelming that it almost made her forget her ambivalence about Jessica. "You know, if Jessica plays her cards right, she could be a cheerleader next year," Mary Ellen said quietly to Olivia, who was bent over, her chin propped on her hand. "She'd probably be the kind of cheerleader you wouldn't even have to worry about breaking in," Mary Ellen went on. She gave an involuntary sigh, thinking what it would be like to have a cheerleading squad that included people as talented as Jessica and Sean. "You know, watching those two out there, I almost envy you, Olivia. It would be great to come back next year just to work with them — assuming they get chosen in the tryouts, that is."

Olivia said, in a voice so low that Mary Ellen almost missed it, "I don't think I'm going to try out for next year's squad, Melon."

Startled, Mary Ellen swiveled toward her. "Olivia! You can't mean that!"

"Yes, I do," Olivia said, staring straight ahead. "I do mean it."

"But why?" Mary Ellen looked worriedly at the crutches. "Is there something you're not telling us about your ankle? Did the doctor — ?"

"No, it doesn't have anything to do with my ankle." Olivia looked at Mary Ellen, her eyes half filling with tears. "I just this minute realized that *all* of you are going to be gone," she said. "I mean, of course I knew it before, but I didn't really *know* it, if you know what I mean. You, Walt, Pres, Angie, Nancy. Everybody I love. You're all going to be gone." She looked away again. "I don't think I could *bear* to work with another team," she whispered. "We're like . . . we're like each other's family, Mary Ellen! How could I stand to have a *new* family?"

Mary Ellen slipped her arm around Olivia. "Yes, I know," she said softly. "But you'll feel the same way about them, after a while." She managed a little laugh. "In fact, I think you'd be pretty lucky. You'd get to have *two* families. Sort of like when parents get divorced and marry somebody else, and you have two bunches of brothers and sisters."

Olivia nodded. "Sure," she said. "But who wants to get divorced?"

Mary Ellen smiled crookedly. "You've got a

point there. Maybe that wasn't a very good way to describe it."

"Anyway," Olivia said, "there's something else." She waved her hand at the group on the floor. "You know, there really *is* some good potential out there. I might not even have a chance, even if I did try out. And it would be pretty awful to try out for the squad and not make it."

Mary Ellen slipped her arm around Olivia's waist. "Hey, cut it out, all right?" she said tenderly. "Listen, don't make up your mind about this right away. This isn't a good time. You're still not feeling up to par and Walt is — "

"And Walt is interested in Jessica in a very major way," Olivia said flatly.

"That wasn't what I was going to say at all!" Mary Ellen exclaimed. "I was going to say that Walt is obviously bothered by something that he hasn't told us about."

"Maybe that wasn't what you were going to say," Olivia observed with a glum set to her mouth. "But it's the truth." She cupped her chin in her hands and stared out on the court, where Walt, who was standing next to Jessica in line, was holding her hand and showing her how to do a sidekick. "They've been like that all day today. I tell you, Mary Ellen, I'm really *not* looking forward to this party tonight."

CHAPTER

Walt's home in the woods — a contemporary log house with floor-to-ceiling windows and a great deck that angled out into the trees — was a terrific place for a party. By the time the rest of the cheerleaders arrived, Walt and Pres already had a huge fire roaring in the fieldstone fireplace that made up one end of the cozy, dimly lit living room. The room was filled with the spicy scent of pine cones blazing in the fire and the snap and crackle of burning pine bark.

Angie, still looking glum, arranged plates of sandwiches and bowls of chips and put them on the big wooden-slab table in the dining room. Mary Ellen, wearing jeans and a red flannel shirt, mixed up several bowls of tangy dips, and Walt took the barbecued ribs out of the oven where they had been heating, heaped them on an enormous tray, and basted them with Bernie's famous barbecue sauce. Pres had brought a large box of tapes for the stereo and was sitting at the kitchen counter, arranging them in the best order for dancing. By the time the preparations were almost finished, the cheerleaders were all in a lighthearted mood, especially welcome after the difficult time they had had with the clinic.

"You know, for a while I wondered if we were going to pull it off," Olivia said, shaking her head.

"Yes," Nancy said, putting the empty chip bags into the trash. "Things really got rough about the time Vanessa showed up." She took off the dish towel she had tied around her waist as an apron. "That girl brings trouble with her every time."

Pres looked up from the tapes he was sorting. "Do you really think she was responsible for what happened at the clinic?"

Mary Ellen looked at Pres in amazement. "How can you even ask such a stupid question, Pres Tilford? Of course she was responsible. I mean, Jessica obviously helped to spread the word — at least, that's what Jessica told us — and I'm sure there were one or two others. But basically it was all Vanessa's doing."

Ardith Engborg walked into the kitchen just in time to hear Mary Ellen's last comment. "Well, you don't need to worry about one thing," she said.

"Oh?" Pres asked with interest. "What's that?"

"I talked to Mr. Howard this evening and explained my concern about any rumors that might appear in the school newspaper. He said he understood, and he would personally read any copy himself before it went to the editor. If there's a problem with Vanessa's story, he'll be sure it's corrected."

"Whoopee!" Nancy shouted, tossing her improvised apron into the air. "Score another one for us!"

Walt leaned his elbows on the counter where Mary Ellen was getting out another bowl. "Do you think Jessica Bennett had very much to do with it?" he asked, in a low voice.

Mary Ellen frowned. "I don't know what to believe," she said. "All I know is that she apologized for passing along something that she heard — from somebody she trusted. Since Vanessa told us that Jessica has been a longtime family friend, I've got to assume that Jessica heard it from Vanessa."

"Yes, but do you think that Jessica deliberately set out to wreck the clinic? I guess that's what I'm asking."

Mary Ellen straightened up and looked evenly at Walt. "Why do you want to know?" she demanded. Was it possible that Walt's interest in Jessica was more than just friendly?

Walt shrugged his broad shoulders. "I don't know," he said. "Just curious, I guess. It just seems . . . well, it's pretty hard for me to believe that a girl like Jessica would do something like that."

"How do you know what kind of girl Jessica is?" Mary Ellen asked, while Walt emptied a bag of taco chips into the bowl.

Walt looked puzzled. "Well, I guess I don't know very much about her, now that you mention it." He grinned. "I guess I'll have to find out."

Mary Ellen shook her head. Walt had always loved puzzles. Sleuth Manners, somebody had called him once, because he had a reputation for getting to the bottom of things. She wondered what his motivation was *this* time.

"I've decided that there's one trouble with this party," Nancy said, coming up to Mary Ellen.

"Oh?" Mary Ellen asked. "What's that?"

"There aren't enough boys," Nancy said, counting on her fingers. "There were only six boys in the clinic and Walt and Pres make eight. But there are fifteen girls, if everybody comes." She laughed a little. "That's almost two to one. That's a pretty uneven number for dancing."

At the mention of boys, Angie looked even more glum. "Well, it doesn't make any difference to me, after what happened today," she said. "Nancy, you don't have to count me. That'll spread the boys a little further."

Mary Ellen whirled on her. "Angie Poletti, are you still torturing yourself over Vanessa's lousy little trick? You *know* there's got to be a good reason for her having Chris's shirt. And you've simply got to put the whole thing out of your mind until you find out what it is."

Angie nodded gloomily. "Yes, I know." She sighed. "I mean, I know that Vanessa will stoop to anything to hurt people. But still — "

She was interrupted by the ringing of the telephone on the wall beside her. Walt came over and picked it up, putting one finger in his free ear so that he could hear. After a minute he held it out to Angie. "It's for you," he said with a conspiratorial grin.

"Who, me?" Angie asked, with surprise. "Who would be phoning me here?"

"Yes, you," Walt said, thrusting the phone at her. "It's Chris. Says he's calling from some motel near Yale, in Connecticut."

Her eyes wide, Angie took the phone and sat down with a thump in the middle of the kitchen floor. Flashing knowing grins at each other, Mary Ellen and Nancy left the room.

"Well, I'm right, aren't I?" Nancy demanded. "About the number of boys, I mean?"

"Yes, unfortunately," Mary Ellen admitted. "But I don't think this is the kind of party where we're supposed to have dates. This is a get-acquainted party, where everybody gets a chance to talk to everybody else. Having a date would kind of get in the way." For a while, she had thought that maybe Pres would be her date to the party. But after the night that Patrick had hit him in the eye, Pres hadn't called. At first, she had been unhappy about it. But after a few days, she had realized that it really didn't matter to her whether Pres called or not. And if that was true, it must mean that their friendship was really only a casual one.

"Well, I wasn't thinking about having a date, exactly," Nancy sighed. "I've still got Eric on my mind, unfortunately. I was just thinking about — "

"Listen, don't worry about there not being enough boys," Pres said, passing them with another bag of ice on his shoulder. "I've invited a couple of extras, just to even things out." He winked mysteriously at Mary Ellen.

"Oh, who?" Nancy called. But at that moment their first guest rang the doorbell, and Mary Ellen pulled her toward the door. "Come on, Nancy, we're supposed to help host this party. Let's go do our job."

The party got noisy and crowded very quickly. The stereo blasted away with Pres's tapes, and the middle of the living room floor was filled, shoulder-to-shoulder, with twisting, dancing bodies. There were some boy-girl pairs, and even a few girl-girl pairs. Everybody was having so much fun, it didn't seem to matter who they danced with.

Mary Ellen was in the kitchen, taking extra sandwiches out of the refrigerator, when she felt a warm hand on her shoulder.

"Dance?" It was Sean, his dark eyes gleaming. "Even the kitchen help gets to have fun sometime," he said, with a kind of practiced persuasion. "And you're way too beautiful to be stuck in the kitchen all evening."

Mary Ellen took a deep breath. Sean really *was* good-looking, in a showy sort of way, and she admired the self-assurance that she could read in his self-confident poise. Or maybe it wasn't self-assurance — maybe it was arrogance, perhaps even conceit. She suspected that sometimes the line between the two was so hazy that even Sean didn't know the difference. "Okay," she said, "as soon as I put out these sandwiches."

The music whirled around them as Sean and Mary Ellen walked out into the living room and melted into the mass of slow-moving bodies. The music was so loud that it vibrated in Mary Ellen's bones, and she was glad that talking was impossible. It felt good to dance to the slow, liquid music. Sean's hand was moving up and down on her back in time to the music in the way that Patrick's hand sometimes did. In fact, with her eyes closed and her cheek against the rough wool of Sean's sweater, she could almost imagine that she *was* with Patrick. She felt a sudden sharp pang of longing for him, so sharp and unexpected that it almost made her dizzy.

"My turn," a deep voice said, over Sean's shoulder.

"Hey, we just got here," Sean protested.

"It's *still* my turn," Patrick said.

Sean started to say something. But then he dropped his arms and stepped aside, shrugging. "Later," he said, with a grin at Mary Ellen.

Mary Ellen stood stock-still, staring. She couldn't speak.

"Thought you could have a party without me, did you?" Patrick asked throatily. He pulled her into his arms.

For a minute, Mary Ellen fought against him, trying to get away. But Patrick just held on, hard. "You — you big jerk!" she spluttered angrily. "Where do you get the nerve to show up here after what you did to Pres?"

Patrick slipped his hand onto the back of Mary Ellen's neck, under her hair. The warm, familiar pressure of his fingers pulsed like a flood through her, and reluctantly she began to relax against his chest. "Pres invited me," Patrick said, his lips against her hair.

"Pres did what?" Mary Ellen pulled back.

Patrick was smiling crookedly. "Yes. I talked to him this afternoon, after the clinic. I . . . I apologized for socking him. And he apologized for taking you out. And then he asked me to come to the party tonight. To even things up, he said."

In spite of herself, Mary Ellen giggled. To even things up! Then she stiffened. "He apologized? *Pres* apologized?"

"Yeah. He said something about you and me and partnerships. I forget exactly what it was." He pulled her more tightly against him and his voice got huskier. "Listen, Melon, do we have to talk all evening? Can't we just dance without all this conversation? I just want to hold you. It's been a long while."

Mary Ellen sighed. Somehow, it all seemed

147

inevitable. No matter how hard she tried to get away from Patrick Henley, he was always there. He couldn't give her the things that she wanted out of life — success, excitement, freedom from Tarenton — but he gave her something else, something that just now made her feel warm and loved. She melted against Patrick, feeling his fingers at the back of her neck, his lips in her hair, his breath tingling her ear. It was inevitable.

Nancy was in Walt's kitchen getting a glass of water, when Sean came up behind her. "How about a dance?" he asked, standing close to her. "I've been watching you all evening, Nancy. You're just too beautiful to be stuck in the kitchen."

Nancy looked up at him. Sean's dark eyes and high cheekbones were interesting — did he have some French in his background somewhere? He was taller than Eric, and less muscular, but he *did* have an attractive face. And he was looking her up and down with undisguised interest. She nodded as he took her hand and they went off toward the living room together.

Olivia was sitting on the sofa, her crutches on the floor beside her. Rock music was blasting from the stereo, people were clustered around the dining room table that was kept filled with food, and the middle of the living room floor was crowded with dancers. Olivia sighed. It wasn't at all strange for her to be sitting on the sofa — without Walt. In fact, it wasn't his usual habit to pay constant attention to her at parties. They had always been comfortable and secure enough to let one another go their own way. And Walt couldn't help being the entertainer that he really was at heart.

Tonight, Olivia saw with a growing nervousness, Walt was *definitely* being an entertainer. And the girl he was entertaining just now was Jessica Bennett. The two of them were standing by the dining room table, eating sandwiches and drinking mugs of cider. And talking. Much to Olivia's discomfort, they seemed to have been talking together most of the evening.

Olivia had found out a little more about Jessica from Monica Rather, a pretty junior from the clinic who had sat next to her on the sofa for a few minutes. Monica had known Jessica for a long time, apparently. It turned out that Jessica's mother worked at Marnie's, and her stepfather had something to do with computers. "Her real father's been dead since she was ten," Monica had said. "I guess that's what accounts for the way she acts sometimes."

"Acts? What do you mean?" Olivia had asked, her eyes on Walt and Jessica.

"Oh, I don't mean she's bad, or anything like that," Monica said hastily, flushing with embarrassment. "I'm not criticizing her, because she's always been a good friend. She just likes to have fun, that's all. She likes to play the field. She always has plenty of dates but she doesn't want to have anyone permanent."

"I see," Olivia said softly.

"Listen, I wouldn't want you to get the idea that I was bad-mouthing Jessica or anything," Monica said, turning even redder. "I really like her. It's just that — "

"No, I understand," Olivia said. "Really I do." In a few minutes, Monica mumbled something about having to get home early and left.

After a while, Pres interrupted and claimed Jessica for a dance. Walt strolled over to the couch and sat on the floor, leaning comfortably against Olivia's leg. They sat in silence for a few minutes, and then Walt put his arm across her knees. "I feel like holding you and you can't dance," he said unexpectedly. "Want to go to the den for a few minutes?"

Olivia swallowed, thinking hard. She really felt like making an issue out of Jessica. She wanted to let Walt know that she didn't like the way he was acting, that his attention to Jessica made her feel lonely and left out. But if she did, would Walt get mad and leave her even more alone? Would he react by being even *more* attracted to Jessica? She decided not to risk it — something unusual for Olivia, who always said exactly what she thought, without counting the possible costs.

"Absolutely," she said. "I'd like to do that." And after a little while, as she and Walt sat snuggled closely together on the couch with only a small lamp lit, she decided that she had made the right choice. Kissing Walt Manners was infinitely better than fighting with him, no matter how terrible she might feel about Jessica. She sighed, pushed the thought of Walt and Jessica out of her mind, and moved more closely against Walt.

Pres came into the kitchen carrying a big plastic bag full of empty soft-drink cans. Ardith Engborg and Mary Ellen were standing beside the sink, cleaning up the last of the dirty dishes.

"Well, I'd say that the get-acquainted party was a great success," Ardith was saying. "I didn't see *anybody* who didn't look well acquainted with everybody else." She stared meaningfully at Pres. "Especially those out on the dance floor."

Pres laughed, thinking about Jessica. They had been dancing together for the last half hour. She was as good a dancer as she was a cheerleader, he thought — light and graceful and responsive. "That's what dance floors are for," he said to Ardith, teasing. "They're for getting acquainted."

Ardith folded up her dish towel, looking reflective. "I know I don't tell you this very often, Mary Ellen, but I was really proud of how the squad members handled themselves today. That was a rough situation, and all of you made the best of it. I know that the last part of the senior year is tough for everybody. But you all are giving it everything you've got and I'm proud of you."

Mary Ellen smiled with pleasure. "Thanks," she murmured.

Ardith looked around. "Well, if that's the last

of the cleanup, I'm going home." She waved at Pres and Mary Ellen. "Good-night. See you at practice on Monday."

After Ardith had gone, Pres glanced at Mary Ellen. She looked very pretty tonight in a funky flannel shirt, he thought. "You and Patrick get along okay?" he asked casually.

A blush spread across Mary Ellen's cheeks. "You might have told me that you'd asked him here," she said indignantly, folding her arms and frowning. "And you might have told me that he apologized to you and — "

"I just forgot," Pres said, grinning. "Did he tell you that I apologized to him, too?"

"Yes," Mary Ellen said. "Why did you think you had to apologize?"

"I didn't *have* to," Pres said. "I just *wanted* to." He put down the bag of cans with a noisy clink. He'd been thinking all evening of how to handle this, but there didn't seem to be any way but one. He had to tell the truth. "Listen, Mary Ellen, I've been thinking. And I've decided that girl friends are pretty easy to get, but good business partners. . . ." He shook his head, grinning. "Well, a good business partner is a pretty rare thing in life. And I'd hate to see what Patrick and I have going broken up over a little territorial dispute."

Mary Ellen raised her chin. "A territorial dispute? That's a disgusting phrase to use about any girl."

Pres laughed, touching his left eye. "I surrender. I'm sorry." He picked up the bag again and shouldered it. "Anyway, I could tell by the way you two were dancing together tonight that I didn't stand a chance," he added. And by the time he had finished dumping the cans and was headed back to the living room where Jessica was waiting for him to take her home, he had convinced himself that it was true.

CHAPTER

13

"Are you ready to leave?" Patrick asked, pulling Mary Ellen's coat out of the closet.

"Yes." Mary Ellen sighed. Patrick had asked to take her home, but he really didn't need to. From the moment he had taken her in his arms, it had been a foregone conclusion.

Walt and Olivia were coming down the hall, Walt with his arm around Olivia's waist, Olivia struggling with one crutch and giggling. Her cheeks were pink and she looked more relaxed and happy than she had all day long. "Are you guys leaving already?" Walt asked.

"As if you cared," Mary Ellen said meaningfully. "I looked all over for you a couple of times, Olivia, especially when it was time to start cleaning up the kitchen. Where *were* you?"

Olivia smiled self-consciously. "Oh, just somewhere," she said. "Did I miss something awfully important?"

"Only if you consider a few dirty dishes important," Mary Ellen replied. "But that's okay. You can make it up later." She laughed. "You can carry all our lunch trays for a week. How's that?"

"It's worth it," Olivia said promptly.

Nancy came up to get her coat. Sean Dubrow was behind her, his dark eyes gleaming in his handsome face. He winked at Mary Ellen.

"Hey, I'm really sorry that I didn't get that dance," he said. "I meant to, but I sort of got distracted." He put his arm around Nancy's shoulder. "You know how it is."

"Nancy, do you have a ride?" Mary Ellen asked, pointedly ignoring Sean. What nerve he had! "If you don't, Patrick and I would be glad to take you home." It would have to be Patrick's garbage truck again, of course. But Nancy had ridden in the garbage truck before and hadn't seemed to mind. In fact, she hadn't seemed to mind riding in the truck nearly half as much as Mary Ellen did. The garbage truck was one of Mary Ellen's chief objections to dating Patrick Henley. Who wanted to drive to the movies perched way up in the front seat of a *garbage truck*, for heaven's sake? And of course, going to the drive-in hamburger place was a joke. The truck was a *real* problem, as far as Mary Ellen was concerned.

Nancy shook her head. "Uh, no, thanks anyway, Mary Ellen," she said, a little awkwardly. "Sean's offered me a ride. He doesn't live very far from my house."

Sean draped Nancy's jacket carelessly across her shoulders. "She's in good hands," he said, with an expressive grin. "You don't have to worry about a thing. You can trust me."

"I'll bet," Patrick hissed into Mary Ellen's ear, as he helped her into her coat. "You can trust him about as far as you can *throw* him."

Mary Ellen laughed, remembering the way Sean had held her when they had danced. If he made the squad next year, he would be a great replacement for Pres, in more ways than one. She thought about Nancy, who in spite of her beauty and her elegant manner was more than a little naive. She hoped that Nancy could handle Sean. It would be interesting to find out from Nancy on Monday just what had happened when Sean took her home.

Just as Mary Ellen and Patrick were walking out the door, Pres and Jessica caught up with them. Pres was holding Jessica's hand and was obviously taking *her* home. But Jessica stood a little apart from him. She looked as if it really didn't matter very much to her if someone took her home, or, she went home by herself.

"Hey, listen, Mary Ellen," Pres said. "There's something I forgot to tell you. Paul Howell called this afternoon after the clinic. He said to tell you that he'd like to see you on Monday after practice. About five, he said. Will that be okay?"

156

"Sure," Mary Ellen agreed, swallowing the excitement that bubbled up suddenly inside her. "That's *great*, as a matter of fact." It had been quite a few days since Pres had taken her to see Paul Howell, and she had wondered over and over again whether she was ever going to hear from him. Monday! Only a day or so more, and she would have some idea about the direction her future should take, about the kinds of things she needed to do to ensure her success as a model.

"Who's Paul Howell?" Patrick asked, as they walked toward the truck parked in Walt's driveway, their feet making crunching sounds on the gravel.

"He's a man Pres introduced me to," Mary Ellen explained. "He's promised to give me some advice about marketing myself as a model." It was a funny thing, she thought. A few minutes ago, on the dance floor, her thoughts had been completely focused on Patrick. Now, at the mention of Paul Howell, that focus had widened a little bit, and she was thinking once more about the future. A future that, unfortunately, could not possibly involve Patrick Henley.

"What kind of advice do you think he's going to give you?" Patrick asked stiffly.

"If I knew that, I wouldn't have to ask him, silly," Mary Ellen said, in a teasing voice. Then she added, in a more serious voice, "He's going to suggest the kind of portfolio I ought to put together, and talk to me about image and stuff like that."

"I don't know why you need any suggestions," Patrick growled. "Your image is just fine the way it is."

"Oh, Patrick," Mary Ellen said, "don't you remember what happened in New York? There are literally *millions* of small-town girls who are trying to get into modeling. I have to be different from all of them. I mean, I have to stand out so that people will remember me. And I can't do that with a high-school-cheerleader image. There's got to be something more. Something special and different."

Patrick sighed as he opened the door and Mary Ellen clambered onto the high seat. "You never forget where you want to go, do you?" he asked quietly and closed the door without waiting for an answer.

"No, never," Mary Ellen said to herself, as Patrick came around the truck and climbed in on his side. "Never, ever."

But when Patrick turned to her in the chilly dark and put his arms around her, she knew it was only partly true. There were certain times in her life when it got awfully hard to remember that her dearest ambition was to be a model, to earn lots of money, to live a glittering and glamorous life. There were certain times, like right now, right this minute, with Patrick's mouth on hers and his fingers tangled roughly in her hair, when she couldn't help feeling that one or two other things in life were pretty important, too. With a sigh, she gave herself up to his kiss.

* * *

"So what happened with you and Sean after the party?" Mary Ellen asked curiously. She and Nancy were standing in the showers after cheerleading practice on Monday, soaking up the hot water.

"Oh, nothing," Nancy said evasively. She turned to rinse herself off.

"Come on, don't give me that 'Oh, nothing' stuff," Mary Ellen laughed. She turned off the shower, basking in the steam. "One look at Sean and anybody could tell that he's a dangerous character."

"Well, he *is* a little pushy, maybe," Nancy said, stepping out of the shower. "But I kind of like that, in a way, if it doesn't get out of hand." She paused, and began to rub herself with a rough terry towel. "Eric is really sure of himself, you know. He's got to be, to be a swim coach. And Ben was like that, too, remember? That was one of the reasons why I loved him. I mean, I don't want to be told what to do, but I kind of like a guy who knows who he is." Her smile was thoughtful. "Anyway, it just felt good to have somebody like me without wanting to *quarrel* with me. It seems like Eric and I have spent most of our time in the last couple of weeks quarreling with one another. Maybe Sean and I didn't have a lot to talk about, but we didn't have a lot to argue about, either."

Mary Ellen nodded. "Yes, I know what you mean," she said slowly, thinking of Patrick. They never really argued, but their basic disagreement, their basic problem, was always there between them. The cold made the goose bumps pop out along her arms, and she hurried to towel herself dry.

"How about you and Patrick?" Nancy asked curiously. "You were together at the party. Does that mean that you're back together again?"

Mary Ellen wrapped the towel around herself and started toward her locker, hurrying across the cold cement floor. "We might have been together, but it doesn't mean a thing," she said, shaking her head. "Nothing's changed." It wasn't strictly true, of course, especially when she remembered how she had felt when Patrick kissed her. And if she let herself be absolutely honest, she would have to say that she couldn't help feeling differently about Patrick after he had socked Pres. Knowing that he cared that much. . . . It embarrassed her to feel that way . . . like a medieval heroine . . . but she did.

"Hello, everybody," Angie sang, dancing into the locker room. "Hello, hello, hello."

"Well, if it isn't little Miss Merry Sunshine." Olivia laughed, turning away from the mirror where she was combing her hair. "You look like you're absolutely drowning in happiness. That must mean that you've solved the mystery of the Wandering Blue-Plaid Shirt."

"Oh, yes," Angie said. "Actually, that mystery got solved on Saturday night, when Chris phoned from Yale."

"So tell me about it," Olivia prompted. "Somehow I missed hearing the details."

"It's your own fault, Olivia," Mary Ellen

teased. "If you had been helping with the dishes the way you should have been, you would have heard Angie's story already."

"Well, it's never too late," Olivia replied. "And as I said, it was worth it. So tell, Angie."

Angie plopped down on the bench. "Well, Vanessa *was* telling the truth when she said that Chris was at her house on Friday night. But she left out a couple of rather important details."

Olivia nodded knowingly. "That's Vanessa. She leaves out all the details that tell the *real* story."

"It turns out that Vanessa's father went to Yale, too, years ago," Angie went on. "So Dr. Barlow and Chris's father are working together to plan some sort of Yale reunion. Vanessa forgot to say that Chris's father was there with him to talk about the possibility of Chris going to Yale." She looked triumphant. "So it wasn't at all the way Vanessa implied. Chris would never have gone over there if his father hadn't made him." She paused and added, "And by the way, Chris told me it was warm in Vanessa's house, so he took his shirt off. He was wearing a T-shirt underneath."

"Ah-ha!" Olivia said. "Score another one for our side." She looked curiously at Angie. "So how was Chris's trip to Yale?"

Angie beamed. "It couldn't have been worse. The plane was late getting into New Haven, and the admissions counselor had forgotten the appointment. It rained all day and they got soaked trying to make their way across campus." Angie wore a delighted smile. "It was a *wonderful* trip!

161

Chris said that his father hasn't even mentioned Yale since they got back."

After listening to Angie, Nancy and Olivia and Mary Ellen convulsed with wild giggles. "I guess it all depends on your point of view," Nancy said at last, wiping her eyes.

"Oh, Mary Ellen, could you come here a minute?" Ardith called, as Mary Ellen came out of the locker room and headed down the hall.

Mary Ellen glanced at her watch. It was after four-thirty, and she was supposed to be seeing Paul Howell at five. She hoped that whatever Ardith wanted, it wouldn't take too long.

"I've got two things to show you," Ardith said, as Mary Ellen came into the office. "First this." She held up a long piece of paper with a list of names written at the bottom of it. "Jessica Bennett brought me this thank-you note after practice today."

Mary Ellen took the paper. " 'Dear Varsity,' " she read aloud. " 'We would all like to thank you for the absolutely *super* clinic you put on for us on Saturday. All of us learned a lot, and we're all looking forward to trying out for the squad. We want to be just as good at cheering for Tarenton as you are. P.S.: And thanks for the wonderful party, too. It was great!' " The thank-you note was signed by all seventeen of the clinic participants.

Mary Ellen handed it back with a smile. "That's really nice," she said. "I know the other cheerleaders will appreciate it, too."

"Yes, it is nice," Ardith said. "The clinic may have gotten off to a rough start, but you and the others turned it around by being so honest and straightforward with everybody." She put the note on her desk and picked up another sheet of paper. "And speaking of getting off to a bad start, I thought you might like to see this, too." She handed Mary Ellen the other sheet of paper. Across the top was typed, in big caps, CLINIC GETS OFF TO A SLOW START, CHEERLEADER SAYS. Under that headline was another one: OLIVIA EVANS DENIES RUMORS OF FAVORITISM. And under *that* was Vanessa Barlow's by-line. Across the typed page, in big red crayon letters, was the word KILL.

Quickly, Mary Ellen scanned Vanessa's feature story. It was just exactly what she had expected, full of innuendoes and half truths about the clinic, implying that the Varsity Squad had set it up so that they could handpick next year's team. Just reading it made Mary Ellen's face flush.

"Don't worry," Ardith said soothingly, watching Mary Ellen's face as she read. "When Mr. Howard saw this, he was really upset and brought it over to me right away for verification. When I told him the circumstances, he killed the story immediately. It's being rewritten by somebody else. And he says that Vanessa won't get another assignment for the paper as long as he's got anything to do with it."

Mary Ellen gave a sigh of relief. "Then it's all over," she said. "Finally."

"It's all over," Ardith agreed, with a grin. She sat down at her desk and leaned back in her chair. "And now that the squad has completely cured itself of the Senior Blues, it's time to get to work again. Don't forget, we've got a game coming up on Friday night. I want to see everybody in tip-top shape."

Mary Ellen looked blank. "Game?" she said. "Friday night? What game?"

Ardith began to laugh. "Go on, get out of here," she said pleasantly. "Before I find myself saying something I'm going to regret!"

"Mr. Howell will see you now," the receptionist said. Mary Ellen stood up and smoothed her plaid skirt. She glanced through the window of Mr. Howell's office. Patrick was waiting outside in the truck, patiently reading a magazine. He looked up and saw her through the window and gave her a thumbs-up signal. She couldn't help smiling. Patrick had finished his route early today, just so he could give her a ride. No matter what her other reservations might be, it was good to know that he was always there when she needed him.

"Well, I'm glad to see you again, Mary Ellen," Paul Howell said, coming out from behind his desk. "Please sit down." He had her portfolio in his hands.

Mary Ellen sat in the same place on the sofa that she had last time. "Well, what did you think?" she asked nervously, gesturing to the portfolio.

164

Paul laid the brown manila folder on the coffee table between them and sat back in the chair, studying her intently.

"I think that these are very good photographs," Paul said. "Most girls, getting started, wouldn't have a portfolio of this quality."

"Do you *really* think so?" Mary Ellen said, surprised. "I didn't think they were very good, if you want to know the truth."

"Well, of course, there's room for improvement," Paul said. "But I would advise you to keep on using the same photographer, if that's possible. He's got a great eye for camera angles and a good sense of composition. If he's not working professionally, he ought to be."

Mary Ellen smiled happily. It would please Patrick very much to hear Paul Howell's judgment about his work. "I'll have to tell him you said that," she said. She waited nervously. Was Paul only going to talk about the photographs? Maybe he didn't think she had much of a chance, and that was his way of letting her down easily. Mary Ellen could feel the muscles tensing up across her shoulders.

"But there's more to be said," Paul said slowly, picking up the portfolio and looking through the pictures. "I think you're an extraordinarily beautiful young woman. I think that you have a great deal of promise as a model."

Mary Ellen relaxed. It was wonderful to hear what he was saying, especially since he wasn't a biased observer, like Mrs. Gunderson or Patrick or any of her other friends. She could trust Paul Howell to tell her the truth.

"But beauty and promise aren't the only things that make a modeling career," Paul went on. "You have a very hard road ahead of you."

Mary Ellen nodded. "I know that modeling isn't easy . . ." she began.

"You just *think* you know that modeling isn't easy," Paul said. He lit a cigarette and blew a cloud of smoke toward the ceiling, leaning back in his chair. "Maybe Pres told you that my sister Elizabeth is a model on the West Coast. She's nearly twenty-two now, and she's just beginning to get good jobs, after years of hard work, years of struggling to get by on almost nothing. And, even though she's a very beautiful woman, Elizabeth is typical. To be a model means to be willing to work eighteen hours a day if you have to. To live on almost nothing for a lot of years." He laughed a little. "Starvation pay, Elizabeth calls it. She says being a model is the best way in the world to ensure that you stick to your diet, because you don't have money to buy many groceries. Until recently, she hasn't even had enough money to come home for the Christmas holidays. And she's been modeling for years now."

Mary Ellen sat up straight, startled. "I knew it would take a while to establish a modeling career, but I thought that I could probably begin getting good assignments after a year."

Paul shook his head. "I want you to write to Elizabeth," he said, "and ask her your own questions. I've written down her address on a piece

166

of paper and put it in your portfolio. I think it would be good for you to get acquainted with a real model so that you can develop a more realistic picture of what's ahead for you." He looked at her sharply. "That is, if you decide to go on with this."

Mary Ellen nodded. "I *am* going on," she said stubbornly. "No matter how long it takes." But for the first time ever, her determination was seriously shaken. Why, she might be better off settling down in Tarenton with Patrick. But she pushed the thought out of her head. "I *am* going on with it," she repeated.

"Well, in that case," Paul said, "I have a very serious suggestion for you." He leaned forward and tapped his cigarette into an ashtray. "I suggest that you contact the Bartlett Modeling School in Chicago, and investigate the possibility of studying there for six months or so. That's the school Elizabeth attended, and she says it made a great deal of difference to her. She says it made her a real pro in the business."

"Modeling school?" Mary Ellen asked uncertainly.

"Sure. They'll teach you about makeup and clothes and posture. They'll help you train your voice, if you want to do television work. And they've got an excellent placement service, so they can help you begin to get jobs." He picked up Mary Ellen's portfolio, leafed through it once more, and laid it back down again. "They'll even help you develop your portfolio and teach you everything you need to know about marketing yourself." He studied her. "What do you think?"

"Would it be expensive?" Mary Ellen asked, thinking about the small inheritance that she had put away in the bank, together with what she had been able to save from her job at Marnie's.

"I think you could manage it financially," Paul said. "Elizabeth tells me that there is a work-study program that would guarantee you some sort of modeling experience while you're learning."

"I'm going to call the school," Mary Ellen said determinedly. "Tomorrow."

"Well, good," Paul said. "I'm glad to hear that. I think it will make a difference to your career." He stood up and held out his hand. "I wish you the very best of luck," he added. "You'll need it."

"Thank you," Mary Ellen said, picking up her portfolio. "I think you've given me good advice."

He looked at her closely and shook his head. "I'm glad that Pres introduced us," he said. "You know, you really are *extraordinarily* beautiful."

Out in the truck, Patrick looked up expectantly. "Well, what did he tell you?" he asked as Mary Ellen climbed in. He put down his magazine and turned on the ignition. The truck shuddered and started with a roar.

"He said your photographs were very good," Mary Ellen said.

"What?" Patrick yelled, over the noise of the engine.

"Your photographs," Mary Ellen yelled back.

168

"He said they were very good. He said that I should keep on using you as a photographer."

Patrick looked pleased. "Really?" he asked. "What else did he say?"

"He said I should go to modeling school," Mary Ellen said, leaning toward Patrick so that he could hear her, "where they would teach me how to do makeup and walk and talk. And how to live on a starvation diet," she added, laughing.

And then she stopped laughing and sat back, thinking about all her wonderful dreams of money and fame and power. She thought of the last year, and the marvelous times she had had as a cheerleader, with Walt and Olivia, Nancy, Angie, and Pres. And she thought of Patrick, too, dear Patrick, who was patient and kind and helpful even when she was being her most willful, most stubborn self. What if *this* year had already been the best year of her life, and she didn't even know it yet?

Patrick switched off the engine and turned toward her. "Listen, Mary Ellen," he said in the sudden quiet, "if it's worth having, it's worth sacrificing for. No matter what you have to give up to get it."

Mary Ellen stared at him. She knew that Patrick wasn't just talking about garbage trucks or the moving business or a modeling career. He was talking about *them*. And when he leaned forward and kissed her gently, she put her arms around his neck, her heart so full that she couldn't say anything at all.

Life was exciting . . . and frightening. The whole squad was approaching new places in their lives. Would they be happy? Mary Ellen couldn't believe they wouldn't be, but how could she be sure?

The seniors are graduating. What will happen to the squad? Read the Super Edition, Cheerleaders #20, STARTING OVER.

Scholastic's Summer Blockbusters!

240-Page Super Edition

TIME MARCHES ON FOR THE CHEERLEADERS®!

STARTING OVER Cheerleaders #20
by Patricia Aks and Lisa Norby

It's up to Olivia to bridge the gap between old and new cheerleaders while Angie, Nancy, Mary Ellen, Walt, and Pres prepare to graduate. But can she do it? Can Olivia forget her anxiety over trying out again for the squad and help the cheerleading candidates who threaten her position? And what about the dark-haired gymnast Jessica whose fantastic ability turns Olivia's boyfriend Walt's head? Time marches on, and Olivia must decide if she's going out for the squad again. But not before heart pains land her in the hospital! Will Olivia ever return to the squad? And, if not, who will carry the torch for the new **CHEERLEADERS**?

0-590-40190-4 $2.50 U.S./$3.50 CAN.

Available in August at your bookstore.

Scholastic Inc.

CHE861

Summer Blockbusters!